THE TWILIGHT OF THE BUMS

Microfiction

Federman/Chambers
Chambers/Federman

with cartoon accompaniment by T. Motley

Book Design: Kevin Thurston. Cover Design: Geoffrey Gatza. General Editor: Ted Pelton.

Artwork © by T. Motley. All rights reserved.

This book was made possible by a generous grant from the Melodia E. Jones Chair of Romance Languages at University of Buffalo.

Acknowledgment is made to the Alt-X Online Network. A different version of *The Twilight of the Bums* appears as an ebook on Alt-X. For more information, go to www.altx.com/ebooks

Library of Congress Cataloging-in-Publication Data

Chambers, George, 1931-
The twilight of the bums / George Chambers and
Raymond Federman ;
with cartoon accompaniment by T. Motley.
p. cm.
Originally published: Boulder, CO. : Alt-X, 2001.
ISBN 978-0-9788811-3-9 (alk. paper)
1. Slackers--Fiction. 2. Older men--Fiction. 3.
Friendship--Fiction. 4. Aging--Fiction. 5.
Experimental fiction. I. Federman, Raymond.
II. Title.

PS3553.H257T85 2007
813'.54--dc22

2007039528

Starcherone Books is a signatory to the Book Industry Treatise on Responsible Paper Use, the goal of which is to increase use of postconsumer recycled fiber from a 5% average at present to a 30% average by 2011.

Starcherone is a non-profit whose mission is to promote innovative fiction writers and encourage the growth of their audiences. Information about the press and our authors, ordering books, contributing to our non-profit, and other aspects of our public-spirited mission may be seen at www.starcherone.com. Our address is PO Box 303, Buffalo, NY 14222.

Table of Contents

For all those who refused to grow up

ONCE UPON A TIME

Once upon a time, and what a screwed up time it was, two old bums met (midway between here and nowhere) and by chance discovered they had the same birth date and the same size shoes, so they decided to be friends. It was a strange encounter, one that seemed predetermined. And it became even stranger when they realized they shared the same shadow, even though one was huge with a Buddha belly, and the other small with an eagle face.

Years went by and it came time for them to die, for as fate decreed, they both had something terminal, and both given at most six months to live. This the two bums accepted but what tormented them was the fact that they had only one pair of socks between them. And so, as friendship dictates, they spent the last six months of their lives each wearing only one sock.

FOOLISH QUESTIONS

How did the bums meet? Dear Reader, you are of a rather cumbersome curiosity. By the Devil what does it matter how the bums met? But if you insist we will tell you that they met by chance, like everyone else.

What are their names? What do you care? Does it matter if their names are Sam & Ace or Um & Laut or Blank & Blank or F & C or Bum One & Bum Two or B Plus or B Minus? They are bums, and that's what they should be called.

Where do they come from? The nearest place. No, that's wrong! The farthest place.

Where are they going? Does one really know where one is going?

What are they saying? Bum One is saying nothing. He is listening to Bum Two who is saying that everything that happens to them here on earth, good or bad, is written above.

AN AMAZING DISCOVERY

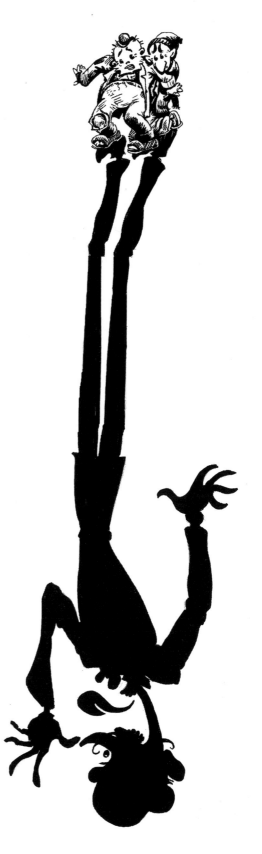

Walking westward down the road one afternoon under a bright blue sky the sun at two o'clock the two bums noticed that only one shadow was cast on the ground for both of them.

How strange! The shadow they flung to the ground with a certain disdain was of one man only though certainly they were two here.

One of the friends (no need to specify which) said to the other: Please, forgive the audacity of such a bold presumption, but I believe we share the same shadow.

Does that mean that I could be you? the other asked, for it was his turn to speak.

The one who spoke first did not reply, but to himself he thought: That depends on your birth date, the size of your feet, and your willingness to share.

THE MIRROR

The old guys are making faces in an old mirror that one of their wives has tossed out. (You understand these guys have wives kids houses mortgages debts careers and so on but that they are bored silly). They are performing heroic busts of military heroes, heroic profiles of the victors, and so forth. Then, at the same moment, they pause, for they have realized that they are looking at each other's reflection. The fat one says, Do you see what I see? The thin one says, Do you see what I see? (You understand these guys are, except in point of birth and sock size, completely different in every regard regarding ethnicity culturicity gonadicity, historicity structuralicity theologicity etcticity). Nonetheless, they continue to stare at each other in the mirror thus exchanging images when all of a sudden the fat one cries out, Sonofabitch, you're starting to look like me!

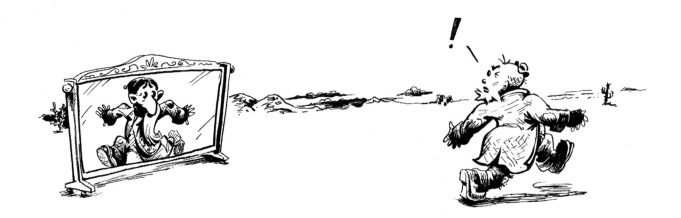

A LOVELY GLITTERY SUNNY DAY

A lovely glittery sunny day ice in the boughs a special glare the old friends sitting on the porch wrapped in blankets are thinking of nothing except the bright sea that bore them to this foreign country.

They are not thinking of all the lovely women they did not fuck nor of all the bucks they did not make nor of all the sausage & pickle kraut they did not eat in their salad days nor are they thinking much of the big smokes they used to smoke nor of those dangerous but exciting days on the front line getting shot at.

No, none of the above. What they are thinking about each in a separate private way, is how much time and energy how much affection and even money they could have saved and stored away had they not wasted all that time energy affection and money on each other.

But then would this be a lovely glittery sunny day?

CONCERNING FRIENDSHIP

The Bums have been friends for so long they have totally forgotten how they became friends, but now that they are approaching the moment when they will have to change tense (this is unavoidable), they often ponder, separately or in unison, this matter of friendship, sometimes in the form of sentences or statements, other times as maxims, or adages, or aphorisms, or proverbs, or pensées, or philosophical propositions, and at other times just words without any form.

We are delighted to be able to present here a dozen of our bums' reflections on the subject of friendship:

1. Do not become friendly with a person inferior to you.
2. To have too many friends is to have none.
3. Friendship is never profitable.
4. A friend must learn to endure his friend's successes as well as his failures.
5. Friends are thieves of time.
6. It is more shameful to mistrust a friend than to be betrayed by a friend.
7. Women may go further in matters of love than most men, but men are way ahead in matters of friendship.
8. A friend is someone with whom you want to do something bad.
9. A friend is there to be abused.
10. When a friend pays you a compliment you can be sure it's bullshit.
11. There are three types of friends: those who love you, those who worry about you, and those who hate you.
12. If a friend can only see with one eye, and as a result wears a patch on the other, always look at him from the good side.

THE BUMS ARE HAVING A DIALOGUE

B 1: I mistrust people who say they have a good memory.

B 2: Did I say that?

B 1: No, you didn't, I'm just speaking in general.

B 2: I prefer when you're specific.

B 1 Okay, but still I mistrust people who ...

B 2: I heard you the first time.

B 1: Alright, alright! You don't have to get up on your high horse.

B 2: And why, may I ask, Mon Cher Ami, do you mistrust those who ...

B 1: It's obvious. A guy with a good memory does not remember anything because he never forgets anything.

B 2: I never thought of that.

B 1: You see what I mean. That's why I do all the thinking and all the remembering for both of us.

B 2: I wouldn't go that far.

B 1: I'll go as far as I want, and if Monsieur doesn't like it he can shove it.

B 2: Now look who is getting pissed.

B 1: You made me forget what I wanted to say.

B 2: You were saying that people with a good memory cannot ...

B 1: Oh yes. Well ...

B 2: But suppose, somehow, the guy who has such a great memory suddenly forgets something, or for that matter everything he knows.

B 1: That's not possible because his great memory would not let him forget.

B 2: Suppose he gets hit on the head by a mugger, or has a car accident and bangs his head on the dashboard, or he falls off a tree and hits his head on a rock, or his wife hits him on the head with a pot because she found out he was screwing around, I don't know, there are so many ways you can get hit on the head.

B 1: Still, it's impossible ...

B 2: Let's say he suffers total amnesia.

B 1: Why do you always have to contradict me.

B 2: Because I'm smarter than you.

B 1: Go to hell!

ON THE RIVER BANK (1)

One day the two old friends were sitting on a river bank each lost in his own thoughts. Friend Number One was thinking about the water in the river rushing playfully before him.

Suddenly he turned to Friend Two and said: Isn't it interesting, mon ami, how one can dip a pail in the river just about anywhere and it will always come up full of the same water, and yet each time the nature of the water is different according to the circumstance of the moment?

Friend Number Two looked at his old buddy and said: Unglaublich, but what you just said is exactly what I was thinking myself.

AN OLD FRIEND

Old age was sitting beside the bums long before they knew him.

Well, you bums, he asked, who's going to get up first?

ANGELS

One snowy day the bums went out rabbit hunting with their friends.
A fresh fall of snow on the already snowy icy ground being perfect for
tracking the little hoppers, wild game makes a delicious winter stew.

Having, at their age, seen quite enough of hunting and killing, but still
feeling sociable, the bums went happily along, but soon fell so far behind
the main hunting party as to lose sight of the pertinacious hunters,
their only evidence being the tracks the bums followed, tracks quickly
disappearing in the fresh fall.

From time to time they could hear far ahead the blast of shotguns, but
these reports were muffled by the distance and the snowfall. The two old
men trudged on silently, each absorbed in his own reflections, disturbed
only by the blasts of the 12 gauges.

Bum one quietly asked the other: Do you suppose we are in any jeopardy? The
main party might circle back and in this low visibility mistake us for hares?

The other considered this, then responded by taking off one glove and
creating the image of a rabbit with his fingers, of the sort one made
shadow figures on a wall, way back in childhood.

Then they trudged on, the snow now at a full, deliberate, serious fall, and a wind beginning to herd the snow into drifts. Suddenly a blast sounded, too close for comfort, and one of the bums dropped to the snow -- I am **shot shot**, he shouted.

Prostrate on his back, in the attitude of death, the one who fell extended his arms sideways in the snow and began to plow it back and forth. With his legs he did likewise.

Are you dying? asked the other, kneeling by his side.

Not yet, was the reply.

What are you doing then?

I am making angels. Go ahead, you too.

The other bum followed suit. He dropped on his back and began to plow the snow back and forth, his arms stiff, his legs stiff, to make a deep secure impression on the snowpack.

This is the sight the hunting party came upon shortly thereafter, their bloodied kill dripping from the baggy game pockets of their shooting jackets.

What a fine rabbit stew to eat that night around the fresh fire in the hunting lodge, and what great stories to tell about the brave hunters, about the game missed, and the game found, and about the two old guys making angels in the snow.

The two angels ... no, the two old bums -- what are we thinking about -- seated side by side, at the head of the table befitting their status, made the first toast, as was their right and privilege: *May this day remind us forever of that which passes. May it remind us, as long as it needs to, of angels, and rabbits.*

ON THE RIVER BANK (2)

One day the two old friends were sitting on a river bank lost in thought in the muddy flow. Friend One was thinking about the water rushing so playfully before him. **Plötzlich** he turned to Friend Two and said: Isn't it interesting how one can dip a pail in the river just anywhere and it will always come up full of the same water and yet each time the nature of the water is different according to the circumstance of the moment?

Two gazed at his old **Kumpel**, considered him up and down minutely, as a tailor measures one for a suit, then **plötzlich**, with no warning, he tossed One in the river, clothes and all, shoes and all, and started shouting obscure slogans by a Marxist philosopher. Whereupon, **plötzlich**, Two grabbed One's ankle and flipped him into the drink, shouting antisemitic curses he learned in school as part of his cultural heritage.

ANOTHER DOZEN OF OUR BUMS' REFLECTIONS ON FRIENDSHIP

1. Friendship knows no gender.
2. One can go fucking with a friend, but friends do not fuck.
3. One cannot fuck a friend, but one can fuck around with a friend.
4. Marriages are established on the basis of similarities, friendships on the basis of differences.
5. Love dies; friendship begins.
6. On sait jamais, say the French, but two do.
7. Friends never tango together.
8. Absence, the mother of most inventions, preserves friendship also.
9. Thirteen? The lucky number of friendship.
10. A friend will put you out of your misery.
11. A friend will remind you that *you said that yesterday.*
12. Friends do not wait.

THE SCORPION & THE CROCODILE

A scorpion wanted to get to the other side of a river. He asked a big crocodile to take him across on his back. The crocodile said to the scorpion, if I take you across on my back how do I know you will not sting me to death? I will not, said the scorpion, because then both of us would sink and drown. The crocodile understood the logic of the scorpion, and so he told the scorpion to climb on his back. While the crocodile swam across the river with the scorpion piggyback, the scorpion stung him. As the crocodile began to sink he asked, why did you do that? Now we're both going to drown and die. I could not help it, replied the scorpion, you see, my friend, it is in my nature to sting, and besides, we are in the Middle East, here life is cheap.

The bums often tell each other symbolic stories. This one was told to Bum One by Bum Two to illustrate a point he was trying to make about friendship and co-existence.

THE PITCHING WEDGE

The two old friends have lost everything except a golf club, a pitching wedge they both use on approach shots, everything else is gone, houses, wives, kids, possessions, golf shoes, golf bag, poof, and since they have only one ball left they take turns shooting. One ball, one club, two men.

Each of these old guys knows that the other likes the approach shot best of all the shots in the game, so there they are staring down at the little ball nicely set up on a nest of strong palmerized fairway special Kentucky mix grass, the ball all white except for the crude red stripe indicating you know what.

One of the friends hands the club to the other saying, Go ahead, you're better at the pitching shot than I am, but his friend shakes his head and says, No, you are, you go ahead, and so friend number one takes the pitching wedge and addresses the ball, but suddenly he gets nervous, he who is known as one of the best pitchers in the county, he is tense because he doesn't want to fuck up the shot and disappoint his friend, so he concentrates on the ball, takes a slow deliberate back swing, but on the way down he shanks the shot, and the ball hops to the right, into the little pond next to the green, plop, and is lost forever.

DESERT STORM

The old guys are bored silly. Let's go live in the hills! So they rent huts in a favela high above the city. Not too close to each other. Not too far from that great outstretched artifact of Xtian imperialism which dominates the landscape. A well between them. One day they both spot a young woman at the well, they rush thitherward with their buckets. Historically, both men are on record as being against all things Xtian and so they know the enemy better than the enemy knows itself, and thus know the text of the parable of the woman at the well quite well. Nonetheless, they scramble down the hill with their buckets. When they are almost at the well, the woman turns around and says to the two puffing sweating old guys: Don't rush, slow down, you'll get a heart attack, and besides, as the old saying goes, when one pail goes down to be filled the other comes up to be emptied. Then she places her bucket on her head and walks away from the two old guys, her hips swaying on the horizon, her hips swaying on the horizon.

SQUALL

A sudden unannounced rush of water from the heavens has driven the occupants of this section of the city park into the shelter, a roof fixed over a few picnic tables. The torrential water is delighting everyone of all ages and all social mix, a veritable babble of folk. Including our two friends, who happen to be in the park tossing a frisbee (underemployment being a serious feature of life among the elderly).

So here is the whole city packed tight by a ferocious rain, a rain from God Itself, and, therefore, as everyone surely knows, to be short-lived.

The rain is so intense, of such ferocity, of such impersonal magnitude (like the idea of God for many of us), that even the most pained or sorrowed members of this sudden group feel free and uninhibited, even playful.

One of the bums is entertaining a bunch of wet kids. He has drawn faces on the knuckles of both hands, and he is playing a little cloak-and-dagger drama with them, which the kids are enjoying immensely, screeching with delight as they watch the knuckle-faces jump up and down confronting each other in a duel to the death, one being the face of the villain, the other that of the hero.

Added to this is the pleasure of the narration, which the bum is uttering in French, in the pure classic French of the Comédie Française, with just the right amount of eloquence and pomposity. Taking on a baritone voice the narrator declaims: *Attention, attention, les enfants, regardez bien, le gentil Petit Poucet va maintenant faire disparaître le méchant Diable.* And suddenly the bum's fingers collapse and make the face of the villain disappear. *Et voila, muscade, disparu*, proclaims the bum. Then changing his voice into that of a soprano, while the Petit Poucet dances proudly before the children, he recites those famous lines spoken by Rodrigue in **LE CID** of Corneille: *Je suis jeune, il est vrai, mais aux âmes bien nées, la valeur n'attend pas le nombre des années.*

No one seems to know this language, but it doesn't matter. In fact, it seems to add to the pleasure as more and more of the fold of the sudden city refocuses toward the bum's knuckles which have made the face of the villain reappear for the second act of this tragedy. (No one knows God too well either, which satisfies all parties, it seems).

The other bum (obviously the one who is not performing) has audienced (what an ugly word) himself to the show, feeling only a slight twinge of envy that it isn't his fingers entertaining the whole city under the big flat umbrella.

Now the knuckles are fighting again, the action is approaching its denouement, the kids are shouting, some mimicking the glorious French language, and then there is one more blast from the water barrel of heaven and just as suddenly a hot sun reappears in the sky, and the whole sudden gathering takes flight, rising as on wings, and flying, flying, away and away, the story left there perfectly unfinished, the way God Itself leaves things, sometimes ...

DARK SHADOWS

No reason why news of the end of the body should be received with anything but acceptance, but for the two bums the news hit hard, especially since they were just at the beginning of their new life in the desert.

The dark hair lovely complexion lady physician in the white coat snapped the x-rays onto the display, and in a gesture that both bums read with private alarm, took off her white coat (although this alarm was confused by the consequent revelation of her body, her generous breasts in a soft semi-transparent brassière, her unspeakable hips). But her act was clearly related to the news, which was not good. She picked up the pointer with the soft rubberish tip, moving from one area of complication to another.

The upshot was the two bums were granted the usual final six months. They looked at each other, then at the lady doctor. They were both thinking the same thought: the two-men-one-girl-thought. The triangle thought. What the hell! Six months is a lifetime if one knows how to take advantage of the unexpected.

AND ONE MORE DOZEN
OF OUR BUMS' REFLECTIONS ON FRIENDSHIP

1. A friend will never tell you that your fly is unzipped.
2. Anything divisible is the enemy of friendship.
3. When a friend tells you what you would rather not hear, don't blame him or her, just tell him or her to shut up.
4. Friendship is not a category.
5. If you fuck your friend your friendship is fucked.
6. He-friend? She-friend? Empty categories.
7. The wine in the broken jug that has been glued back together always tastes better; likewise with friendship.
8. A friend lets you crack open his or her fortune cookie.
9. Friends are nuts.
10. One of the good things about friends is that they come when called. The other good thing is that they leave.
11. One of the pleasures of friendship is to be in the state of missing that person.
12. Making lists of the qualities of friendship is like eating salted peanuts.

OLD POLISH PROVERB

The two old friends are living proof of the old Polish proverb that a good friend will wipe his shoes on you.

One time the Mick fobbed off a lovely looking chick on the Frog telling him what a great lay she was when in reality her cunt was cement.

Another time the Frog told the Mick he had met this lovely and ready virgin who was asking for immediate defloration and that he wanted him to do it to her, but when the Mick's anxious cock approached the virgin's sweet cunt it discovered that it was not, as announced by the Frog, an unexplored path in a virgin jungle but rather a well traveled superhighway where many good cocks had already crashed.

THE BIG SHOOT-OUT

One day the two old shoeless bums came into town with a plan for making a few bucks, getting some shoes, a meal, and maybe a 2-for-1 lay at the local brothel if there was one. It was cold & snowy, lucky they each had greatcoats in pretty good condition. So at the town gate they split up, one going north & the other south. At the north bar Old Bum One slammed down his fist on the table & said he was in town to kill his enemy at noon on Main Street. At the south bar Old Bum Two shouted the same threat, looking down at his coat as if to suggest he carried a weapon. As you can imagine, this news traveled about town at the speed of excitement. When was the last time, if ever, that the town had witnessed a shoot-out? And so as noon approached the entire population of the town assembled on Main Street. Everybody was there, the old, the young, the crippled, the rich, the poor, the unemployed, the bosses, as well as the town politicians, and even the blacks from the ghetto.

When it was past noon, and the old shoeless bums had not yet arrived for the big shoot-out, the people started getting restless. One could hear rumbling in the crowd. The town sheriff dispatched one of his deputies to find out where the two bums were, that's what he called them, **bums**! Soon the deputy came back. He looked horrified. He had located the two shoeless bums at the local brothel, both fucking the same girl at the same time, one frontward the other backward, yes that's what the deputy reported, one into the front the other into the rear at the same time. They had her sandwiched. Then the deputy added, from the look of them two bums, there'll be no big shoot-out today, and probably not for the rest of the week.

THE WOMAN OF GREAT RESISTANCE

There was on that gloomy day only one woman left in the world with sufficient inner resistance to stiffen male power to a structure sufficient for her use to ensure the continuity of the species.

There were also on that day only two nameless bums left, two good-for-nothing thieving trash-hackers fucking worthless drunks suspended on their crosses.

And so on that gloomy day the woman of great resistance drove her donkey cart up to Golgotha, the place of skulls and olive trees, to inspect the men slowly crucifying in the heat of mid-day.

Noticing the dust on the trail Bum One said from his high perch: I see something coming. Bum Two lifted his head, and through the dust cloud he saw the outline of the donkey cart. It's a little early isn't it? he said, thinking it was the cart from the mortuary on its way to collect their corpses.

History does not record what happened that day on Golgotha when the woman of great resistance climbed up the cross, but perhaps one can get a clue from the words Saint Augustine scribbled in his Confessions:

Do not despair, one of the thieves was saved.
Do not presume, one of the thieves was fucked.

THE PRINCESS & THE FROG

Once upon a time, and what a scary time it was, the two friends got lost in the woods and were just about starved when a fairy princess leapt out of a pond and offered herself to the men, who were still quite young, little more than boys really. Necessity offering no other option, they ate the princess on the spot, as bid, and were restored enough to make their way out of the woods to a human settlement. Many years passed and the boymen all but forgot the princess who had saved their lives until one day the two friends, now old men, were fishing in a pond when a frog leapt out of the water. Oh what a big fat frog, one of the friends cried out. Hey, why don't we have frog legs for lunch, said the other friend. So they caught the frog, proceeded to dismember it, cooked the legs on their portable camping stove, and soon delighted in the savory flesh, not realizing that only a kiss from them would have transformed the frog into a beautiful fairy princess.

A LITTLE REQUEST

In the long run in the scheme of things what kinds of things do you want a woman to do for you? He asked his friend.

And the friend replied, as things stand now with the old bones weeping and the muscles creaking I would like a woman to kneel before me and tie my shoe laces.

EXCHANGING VIEWS

Um: I would like my spouse to serve me a meal

Laut: I would like my spouse to cook me noodles

Um: I would like my spouse to watch tv with me

Laut: I would like my spouse to play games with me

Um: I would like my spouse to be home for me

Laut: I would like my spouse to respect my
       private mail

Um: I would like my spouse to hear what I'm saying

Laut: I would like my spouse to understand
       my poetry

Um: I would like my spouse to replace the cap
       on bottles

Laut: I would like my spouse to stop using
        talcum powder

Um: I would like my spouse to go sleep in
       another bed

Laut: I would like my spouse to stop snoring at night

Um: I would like my spouse to end her childhood

Laut: I would like my spouse to stop
        cultivating senilities

THE SOCIOLOGY OF WIFEHOOD

The wife is the woman you end up with who is neither your mother nor your mistress. She's the one who visits your sickroom every day, and when you complain to her that you don't want to be there she replies that she doesn't either. The mistress and the mother cannot be lived with, they can only be visited. But the wife is the woman you live with, as she lives with you, and not with her father or her young lover with the thick hair and the slick mustache. She is the one who brings you clean socks and fresh underwear, who double-checks your checkbook figures, and has just a few weeks ago completed the plans for the removal of your body. Then, as she leaves, she bends to kiss you, and you look up to receive her smooch, knowing that her dear face is the one you'll see first tomorrow, if you make it, and even if you don't.

The above material Bum One has just read to Bum Two, implicitly seeking his opinion. Two shakes his head soberly, affirming both the justice and the insight of the prepared remarks. Awesome, he says, snapping the paper with his fingernail, but don't show it to Sophie.

A DELICATE SITUATION

Our situation is truly delicate, Bum Two told Bum One as they set out one morning for the day's occupations. What I mean is this: What fine things, what momentous things, are we going to miss through fear, fear of falling back into the old errors, fear of not finishing in time, fear of reveling, for the last time, in a last outpouring of misery, impotence, and senility.

To which Bum One replied calmly: Don't worry like this. The forms are many in which Bums like us can seek relief from laziness.

THE AGING PROCESS

As one ages one tends not to become richer or wiser or kinder, etc., no. There tends, rather, simply to be more of what one is. We mean the character thing. This, for example, Bum A is showing forth as a frustrated infant in perpetual rage, whereas Bum B is developing into a destructive fourteen year old. This is as far as both of them got in the character development department.

So we find them on this day flying along coastal highway 101 north of Los Angeles in a snappy rental convertible, its top down, the boombox blasting Shostakovitch piano preludes, when suddenly Bum A says, I gotta go pipi! Bum B doesn't react and continues to speed up the highway. If you don't stop, whines Bum A, I'll pee in my pants. Bum B rather than slowing down presses harder on the accelerator and cries out into the wind, You're a real baby, you know! Okay, I'll stop as soon as I see the proper tree, meanwhile cross your legs and shut the fuck up so I can listen to the music.

PENNIES IN HEAVEN

Um & Laut are flying somewhere. On U.S. Air. It's a long flight, but we cannot tell you where they are going because the bums themselves don't even know why they are on this plane. They are bored. They have already seen the dumb movie that is being shown (HOME ALONE), they have read all the magazines, and they don't even feel like flirting with the flight attendants. Air hostesses used to be sexy and pleasant, but nowadays they all seem well past their prime and indifferent to the needs of the passengers. Anyway, Um & Laut are bored. Sleep is also out of the question because they have already slept for a couple of hours (old men never sleep more than a few hours at a time).

Let's play a game, says Um.

What kind of game? inquires Laut.

Let's see how far we can count numbers, suggests Um.

Hey, that's not a bad idea, agrees Laut, but let's do it this way. We take turns counting, but each time we double the numbers.

What do you mean?

Well, you say 1, I say 2, then you say 4, and I say 8, and you say 16, so on.

Okay. You begin.

U:	1
L:	2
U:	4
L:	8
U:	16
L:	32
U:	64
L:	128
U:	256
L:	512
U:	1024
L:	2048
U:	4096
L:	8192
U:	Are you sure, it's 8192?
L:	Yes, I am. My dear Um, you know I never make mistakes with numbers. Go on. This is fun.
U:	16384
L:	32798. No. I think I made a mistake. It's 32768. Yes, 32768
U:	65536
L:	131072
U:	262144
L:	524288
U:	1048576. Wow, I never had so much fun in an airplane. Don't stop. Keep going.
L:	I am, dammit. 2097152
U:	4194304
L:	8388608
U:	16777216
L:	33554432
U:	67108864
L:	
U:	Well, what are you waiting for?
L:	I have to rest a moment. I'm out of breath.
U:	That's the problem with you. You're out of shape. You don't exercise enough. I keep telling you, you've got to exercise, or you're gonna become a decrepit old fart.
L:	Okay okay. I'm fine. What was the last one?
U:	67 million 108 thousand 8 hundred and 64
L:	
U:	Come on already!

L: Don't rush me. 134217728
U: 268435456
L: 536870912
U: Wait a minute, you're going too fast.
L: Aha, now look who is out of shape.
U: It has nothing to do with that. I just want to make sure I don't make a
     mistake. I mean if you're gonna play the game you're gotta play it right.
L: Then play, and stop yapping.
U: Alright. Where were we?
L: Shit! I forgot now.
U: No big deal. Don't get excited. We have all the time in the world.
     Let's start all over again. But this time let's really keep it going.
L: Okay. My turn to start. 1
U: 2
L: 4
U: 8
L: 16
U: 32
L: 64
U: 128
L:
U: Well, are you already out of breath?
L: No no, I just thought of something. Something incredible.
U: In the middle of the game! Alright, what's your big thought?
L: Imagine how rich we could be today if for one month, one month
     only, a mere thirty days, we would have saved one penny the first
     day and then doubled the amount every day after that.
U: How rich would we be?
L: Multimultimillionaires, you idiot. Didn't you see how fast these
     numbers add up?
U: Hey you're right. We would have millions and millions of pennies.
     How many dollars are there in 3435977632 pennies?
L: That's easy. 34 million 359 thousand 7 hundred and 76 dollars
     and 32 cents.
U: Wow!
L: Isn't that incredible?
U: Hey, Laut, I have a idea. Why don't we start saving right now? I give you
     a penny today, and tomorrow you'll give me two, and the day after tomorow I'll
     give you four, and by the end of the month we'll be multimul...

**Ladies and gentlemen the captain has turned on the safety belt sign
in preparation for our landing ...**

BOCCACCIO

The Old Bums, as you know, share a shadow. And so, when the sun is out, they take turns wearing it -- what are friends for? This fact doesn't seem to have much to do with the great wop storyteller, but you just wait.

The Old Bum on your left is telling the Old Bum on your right a B tale which the right Bum is receiving with growing resistance, if not outright incredulity.

No shit, mon cher, Leftie continues, the guys switched wives, the girls couldn't tell the difference.

I find this hard to believe, responds Rightie, I think you are preparing me to suggest that we switch wives, that is the real burden of your tale.

Alors, ça non, replies Leftie, on the banks of the very Seine whereupon I was born, I swear that I do not lie!

You liar! shouts R, heating up. You want to lie with my delicious young wife, whose breasts even braless retain the vibrant shape of youth and passion, whose Segovia guitar hips rival the hips of ...

Forgive me for interrupting you, île de rêve, but you mean **lay** not **lie**.

See what I mean! This proves it! You want my wife!

This little exchange does prove indeed that words and deeds do not always coincide.

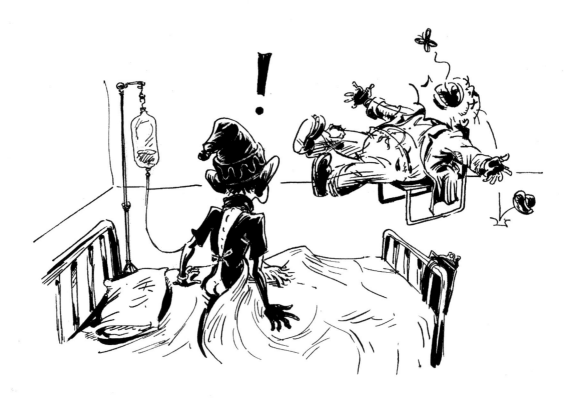

IN THE HOSPITAL

As it inevitably happens to old farts, one day one of the two friends fell ill. As he lay on his hospital bed dozing, the other friend came to visit. Since Old Fart One seemed asleep, and Two didn't want to disturb him, he quietly sat by his bed in a chair, and soon fell himself into deep sleep.

This is what Fart Two told himself in his dream: We've been through strange and wondrous things together. Unwittingly you and I sipped our fill of joy and bitter woe from the cup of life. And now that it's almost empty, one might be tempted to believe all that was only a test, and that now fortified with the wisdom of experience, we stand before the real beginning. This is the real beginning, and though we do not wish the return of past delusion, we are happy to have lived it as it was. And so I now feel confident that whatever ill attacked our old friend, he will soon be doing better than before.

While the voice inside sleeping Fart Two continued to rant, Fart One regained consciousness, and seeing his friend asleep in the armchair, quietly snoring, his face twisted into a painful grimace, he reached out and shook him, Why don't you get in bed with me, you Old Fart, you don't look well at all.

THE SEX NURSE

You don't have to be a sick man to experience the fantasy of the Sex Nurse. Every man in trouble imagines that a woman much like his mother or his mistress is coming momentarily through the door to slip under the sheets with him and restore his pricky manliness.

Our friends are no exception.

One in the chair and Two in the bed, they've been holding hands, snoozing, dreaming of her, all in holy white. So, when she does appear, carrying, like a waitress, a tray of tiny fluted paper cups of pills, Sex Nurse Herself, pausing by the bed, double-checking the pill cups, her freshly laundered white uniform so sweet and clean smelling, oh, oh it's spring and a window flies open, her uniform embracing and defining her naked womanhood, and so on and so forth, the old guys waken, their handclasp tightening, tears inching down their cragged, manly faces.

THE SKY BOX

The two bums, the guys we often speak of, the ones who share a birth date and a sock size, and a shadow, are also men, through no fault of their own, of a defined substance in the secondary community in which they live and work. Their wives enjoy their status in this community and have, as wives are wont, ambitions beyond their state. And so it is that at the class AA ballpark one may view, much to the chagrin of the bums, a structure just above the bleachers, where the wives come to entertain their friends and view the games in air-conditioned comfort.

On the day in question, an interesting game is on-going, scoreless, bottom of the third. The bums are seated in the proletarian green bleachers directly below the sky box, a gesture to the masses they insisted on. The bums are sitting just behind a youngish woman, an up-and-coming lawyer, they decide, who is studying the game with a total attention that frees them to view with delight her appetizing derrière which bounces with every move and every shout she makes to encourage her favorite players.

Bottom of the third then. This is what they are doing. But it's also her fingers, their slimness, and the way the shaped nails sit on them, which attract the bums' attention. They are having sex fantasies about these lovely slim fingers, which rest composedly on a legal pad, but also her thick bush, a miracle of Levantine black, and the revealed scalp beneath it so healthy, so clean. Those lovely fingers, her healthy hair, and that appetizing derrière, the two bums have lost interest in the game.

The wives, meanwhile, sit in the circle of easy chairs at the back of the box, chatting with their invited guests, the wives of the police chief, the mayor, the school superintendent, the guest conductor of the local symphony orchestra.

But now, it's the seventh inning stretch. The two bums get up to stretch with the rest of the crowd and so does the lady up-coming-lawyer who turns to view the crowd behind her thus facing the two bums. Oh my mamamia! What a set of boobs. Unbelievable. These generous protuberances will no doubt occupy our two bums, along with the rest of the lady's anatomy, until the end of the game, and will probably prevent them from enjoying the local team's victory.

CHEZ MONETTE

One day Monette invited the boys to tea to meet Henri, her newest conquest -- a large man with a thick beard (big and thick enough to store things in, oh say a pipe cleaner kit) and big opinions (quite natural for a pseudofrog).

This, you are thinking, is indeed an auspicious opening. You wonder why the guys hate Henri so.

Monette, it should be revealed, did time as the mistress of the bums (not the same sentence, of course -- social *bienséance* must be preserved).

Ah, we see, so the bums are still in love with the memory of Monette and resent their reincarnation in Henri.

Right you are. Henri is standing (he likes to be upright for his major utterances, *avec un accent, bien sûr*) near the delicate tea table with its fine Limoges service, a pleasant little stream of steam rising from the pot, a pot deeply glazed, a white crane -- the ancient symbol of longevity -- depicted in the attitude of flight.

The boys are seated together on what is called a love seat *[hey, specify that it is an original Beauvais, whispers my co-author]*. You may be sure they detest it.

(Oh, lest we be accused of not reporting the scene faithfully, we must mention here, especially since it is an important detail, and a nice touch, the record-player, next to the love seat, on which Monette is playing her favorite recording of Mireille Mathieu singing **Je m'en fous!**) *[Hey, did you mention the pipe that Henri is holding in his hand? Yes, my co-author again.]*

Monette is reclining on a curious bit of furniture (hard for us to tell what it is from where we are), a sofa of sorts, elevated at one end, on the bolsters of which she is carefully, most piquantly semi-reclined, her camellia gown draping, its folds flowing and draping, flowing and falling, and falling *[you're pushing, keep the effusions down. Oh shut up, let me go on]*.

Henri is working it up, his major new thought *[une pensée cartésienne*, to be sure] on the Fall Of Rome (he capitalizes his opinions).

I, he begins, the word in his register one endless vowel. **Iyeeeeeeee**

Whereupon enters Bum Two, aka **Blitz**.
Who, Monette ma chérie, was your most superior lover?

Blitz, of course, speaking in this manner, nominates himself *[bien entendu]*.

Hmm, responds Monette, wishing, perhaps, that she had a fan to shield her face at this moment. *[Hey, nice touch the fan!]*

Henri is taken aback (he has the look of a musketeer who has just been touché). Bum One enters, **Tell us do, dear Monette, which one it was who touched your sacred source, the font of your essence.**

Henri returns to the plate. After a long drag in

and a slow puff out on his pipe, **Do**, he commands, **do it**.

Gosh, poor Monette is on the spot, eh? Do you think she is enjoying this? Perhaps you even think she expected to sit on this hot seat? *[Stop asking the reader to think, it's dangerous.]*

Ah, begins Monette, somewhat shyly, almost in a whisper *[Wow, there's a lot of whispering in this thing]*, **One was gymnastical, but recited the loveliest poetry as he worked me over, something like** un cube sur un cube cela fait deux cubes, deux cubes sur deux cubes cela fait un mur entre toi et moi, et toi tu es là tout gras en train de manger ta soupe, **a poem that Juliette Greco, I recall, performed in one of those existentialist movies set in North Africa with that Brit of a Brit as hero, I forget his name, his face is horribly pocked. Tea?**

The men at this moment are experiencing profound regret for having permitted any floor space at all for the question which elicited Monette's response. *[Watch your syntax, still whispering in my ear, you know who.]*

Monette pours the tea, **Hmm**, it has a saffronish quality, somewhat unarticulated. The tray of tiny cakes *[make it French pastries]* ... the tray of *petits fours* she then nudges toward the men (Henri having repositioned Himself behind the loveseat, next to the record-player -- we told you the record-player would play an important part in this).

But, continues Monette, softly, **ultimately, I felt like a grip on a horse, you know, one of those hand-grips on stationary horses -- how do you call these horses? -- which gymnasts do their stuff on. Now, as to the next one in question, I have a most curious response, a response I will make as plainly as I can. He was a wonderful lover I am sure no doubt, to be sure, but being with him was like being alone. I speculated, if I may say so, that he loved me profoundly, so utterly, that he quite disappeared within the force-field of my Being, if that doesn't seem too farfetched.** *[Which of the bums do you think she is alluding to?]*

Do you suppose, dear Reader, that at least one of Monette's guests is regretting having accepted her invitation to tea?

The men have stiffened considerably, Henri stark in his Gallic uprightness, the boys on the upholstery sinking back, which movement most unfortunately brings them closer (do you understand here the design of the love seat? -- if not, hurry now to an appropriate information source before continuing).

Bum Two interposes, **Gentlemen, how many seconds of consciousness does a** person have after the blade of the guillotine has done its work?

The third lover, Monette now speaking with some confidence, a bit louder, refusing utterly the last question, not about to be chopped off, **now there was the Summun Bonum!**

The Summun Bonhomme? gasps Henri, unwittingly.

The Summun Bonem! utter the bums on the love seat, as one.

Yes, yes, yes, says Monette, **yes, yes. The Bonum. The Summun. What more can one say? Cake?**

What a delicious moment, eh dear Reader? Can you taste the silence that ensued? Could we extend beyond this point?

[We doubt it.]

A SERIOUS DISCUSSION

Ace: Tell me Sam, do we have a goal? Did we ever have a goal?

Sam: My dear Ace, our goal, if we ever had one, was to say less, to say badly whatever we had to say, or if you prefer to unsay what had already been said.

Ace: Do I hear you correctly? You're saying that the goal of our being on this stinking planet, was not to say, but to say less?

Sam: Exactly! Or to put it in simpler terms, all I'm saying is, shut up, and don't ask dumb questions.

[two hours later same day]

Ace: Are you sure?

Sam: Sure of what?

Ace: Sure that we didn't have a goal.

Sam: You're impossible, you know. Here you go again.

Ace: I just want to know.

Sam: Let me say it one more time for the last time. Our goal, if we had one, was less to advance, less to go forth -- to progress in other words -- than to delay.

Ace: In what sense, delay?

Sam: In nonsense, you cretin!

Ace: Okay, okay, don't get excited, but somehow we've managed to come that far.

Sam: Oh yea! What far! Where?

Ace: Where we are now.

Sam: Sometimes I wonder how I've been able to endure you all these years.

Ace: [wipes a tear]

Sam: I'm sorry. One more time. Our goal was not to clarify, but to obscure, to make things darker. Do you get it?

Ace: Oh, I see. To make things less clear! ... Did we succeed?

Sam: Of course we did.

Ace: Then I feel much better.

THE COSTUME BALL

For the first time since they moved to Bumsville, more than forty years ago, the bums have been invited to attend the annual fund-raising costume ball to be held the County Museum of Modern Art.

The invitation stressed: **Come dressed as your favorite fantasy.**

For lack of space in this literary effort, we will not describe what the wives of the bums wore for the occasion, we will simply say that they both looked very attractive in their movie star costumes. As for Bum One, he went dressed as a Ku Klux Klan. He had shaped a white sheet into a long hood that came down to his ankles, and in it he had cut two eye holes. It was not bad, though he looked more like a cute little ghost than a mean ugly Klansman.

Bum Two went disguised as a Neo-Nazi Skinhead. He had shaved his head completely, put on huge iron-cross earrings and a chain necklace. He was bare chested, wearing only black leather pants with suspenders, boots that reached up to his knees, and on his fingers rings shaped into human skulls. On his forearms he drew SS tattoos, and on his chest he pasted a large photograph of Adolf Hitler.

The bums were a sensation at the ball. In fact, Neo-Nazi Bum won first prize for his costume (a magnum size bottle of California Champagne), and Ku Klux Klan Bum was awarded second prize (a regular one liter size bottle of New York State Champagne). [We apologize for the stinginess of the prizes, but Bumsville is at this moment in the midst of an economic crisis.]

Walking home a bit tipsy after the ball (still in their costumes), Bum Two embraced his friend and congratulated him for having won first prize, but he said, with a slight tone of envy: You know, I don't understand how a Neo-Nazi Skinhead can appear more important to the judges of this contest than a Klansman.

Oh, that's obvious, replied the winner, right now the Klan is in decline, whereas Neo-Nazism is on the rise. But you don't have to be a sore loser because of that.

50

A CURIOUS ARRANGEMENT

When the bums landed in Warsaw on their tour of East European countries, they took a bus to the edge of town and started thumbing to Krakow about 240 km south, the Mick out in front, the Yid hiding in the brush, in ditches, behind trees, taking cover wherever available.

There are historical reasons for this curious arrangement, this necessary precautionary situation. Tell us, O Fable, when there were no such reasons.

THE TURNCOATS

Between them the bums can speak and/or understand Turkish, French, Erse, Japanese, Latin, American, Javanese, German, British, Italian, Hebrew, Dutch, Spanish, Yiddish, and even Ladino, that lovely little language which the Sephardim invented after they were kicked out of Spain a few times ago. But none of these have worked. The bums are lost in a big city, and no one has any idea what they are trying to say, it's a bad dream.

They make a hand gesture which they believe is the international sign for being lost, for distress, but from every person in this city to whom they perform this gesture all they get in return is the bite of the thumb, a gesture they do not understand a fig.

It is not understand a fig.

What is then, Schmartie?

It is give a fig.

What does it mean?

Dunno.

The old bums are lost, they are lost and tired. They are lost and tired and hungry. They are lost and hungry and thirsty and tired.

Fooled you, didn't I?

What?

Fooled you, didn't I?

You already said that.

You expected a certain order based on expectation in the last run of sentences, didn't you?

I am tired and thirsty.

We're lost.

The bums sit on a bench. What a lovely city, a small city somewhere, it looks like the western Argentine. What a lovely city, a small city somewhere in the Argentine, or in the Crimea, or in the Persian Alps. But still, provincial beauty notwithstanding, they cannot make themselves understood. And every time they try, the folk bite their thumbs.

The smaller of the two bums takes off his coat, turns it inside out and puts it on again. Looks ridiculous, all the bits of stuffing and loose thread and stitching are exposed. You do likewise, he says to the fat bum. Turn your coat inside out.

But it is embarrassing, and very uncomfortable.

Do it anyway, my mama told me a story once about a lost kid who did this.

So, what happened to him?

I don't know, she died before she could finish the story.

That fast?

It was a long story.

Oh, well then. Fat Bum turns his coat inside out while Small Bum steps behind the bench to reverse his trousers.

There they sit then, dear Reader, the inside-out gang, our two lost bums, two turncoats on a bench somewhere on earth. What do you suppose happens next? Or do you suppose the bums are already saved? It is up to you to finish the tale.

STEP-MOTHERS

The bums are, we have been informed, on their farewell tour of selected cities of the European continent. They have said goodbye to Prague and so long to Vienna. In Madrid, they uttered the same sad farewell they uttered the last time they were banished. Today we find them in Berlin of all places. In, of all places, the Botanical Gardens.

In the Gardens, the old men have come upon a presentation of pansies, a special display of pansies, thousands of tiny faces, living souls of the dead, their colors intense under indirect artificial light, a violent intensity in the blossoms and in the air itself, as if ghost petals extended limitlessly, superblack extension of the fragile velvety petals, the whole vibrating under a huge hand-painted sign in old High Gothic script:

STIEFMÜTTERCHEN

Then something happens. Something that we can only approximate, that we can only suggest. It happens like this.

One of the bums suddenly turns to the other, and asks if he remembers a visit they made to a botanical garden in another city, years and years ago.

The other bum replies that he does remember that visit. In fact, he remembers clearly that it was a display of Easter lilies that attracted their attention then, huge white trumpets, and a smell, almost sickening ...

The first bum closes his eyes and asks the other bum to lead him through the field of **stiefmütterchen**, the delicate glowing banks of **step-mothers**, as they are known to us English speaking folks.

The blind man puts out his hand, the other knowing to guide it toward a blossom. The blind man feels the blossom, the tender stalk, the fragile hardy insistence of the plant.

Close your eyes too, and feel, he says to his friend. But already his friend is groping with the palm of his hand into a cool bed of peat moss.

My mother had no place for bedding plants in the little courtyard in front of our house, says the blind man, but I'll bet she imagined flowers like these ... strange they are called step-mothers.

Why, wonders the other man, equally absorbed, do I think we had a blind gardener?

Everything died with her when she was ... all her beds of flowers, her forsythia, her roses, her tulips, her iris, her gladioli ...

Then the first blind man says, remember, we were in Kyoto, trying to find this place we had heard of where you could get a good whole body massage, a delicious massage, better than a fuck, we were in Kyoto, we were the occupying forces, you know, and we were stumbling about the place looking for this special massage parlor, when we entered a part of the city, a restricted zone, a zone of blind folk, all wearing white cotton kimonos, a zone of survivors who had been blinded by the radiation blasts at Hiroshima and Nagasaki, a zone of blind people stumbling along trying to make their way through the narrow streets of their ghetto. So many sightless folk in those flowing white cotton kimonos ...

Why am I telling you this? We didn't want a massage anymore. We went back to the base.

Yes, I remember. And soon after that you lost your mother, says the other bum.

Thus relocated in such a steep absence, the old men open their eyes, and for an instant the light and the bright colors of the pansies make their eyes water, and now they are ready to bid farewell to another city they will probably never see again.

WISLAWA SZYMBORSKA

So the boys are now in Krakow trying desperately to find the reclusive poetess Wislawa Szymborska to ring her up and announce to her that two of her greatest fans have shuffled all the way from Bumsville, as it were, and wish to chat with her, to take her to lunch and a ride on the ferry (if there is one in Krakow).

The rattlesnake approves of himself without reservations, is the bums' favorite line, a line we find them chanting aloud over and over again at the Café Milo_z Szcze_liwa while eating boiled potatoes and drinking vodka, and where the other patrons look at them as their own future, as what they will become when they too are rich American fuddy-duds, as their beloved homeland becomes yet another anonymous market economy.

What, inquires Boy 1 of Boy 2, does the rattle-snake approve? Then they both chant the answer to the question, which we now invite you also, dear reader, to sing along with them: *The rattlesnake approves of himself without any reservations.*

Where is this literary effort going, where is Wislawa Szymborska? Why doesn't she answer her telephone? Where are you Wislawa, dear? Why won't you reveal yourself and come dine with the old rattlers, whose tails knock so hollowly in such unreserved approval.

What to do, where to go, how to proceed, what surface other than the poem to inhabit. The boys order more boiled potatoes and another round of vodka (yes, beloved reader, yes indeed) and start chanting another Wislawa line:
We see here an instance of bad proportions, we see here an instance of bad proportions.

REPROBATION

Bum One[alias Um]:
Is it clear to you my dear Laut that our friendship is the only light & joy in this miserable life of mine? That the rest is gloom, despair, anguish, rejection, silence, repulse, disgust, hammering anger, wretched shunning, unchecked desperation, aggressive paranoia, psychotic anxiety, reactive depression; that except for our friendship, I am lost in the hills and valleys of neurotic anguish which I helplessly manage by mirroring; that I am located exactly in the place uttered by the mud of nothingness.

Bum Two [alias Laut]:
You know Um sometimes you really get on my nerves, I am fed up with all your gloom, despair, anguish, rejection, silence, repulse, disgust, hammering anger, wretched shunning, unchecked desperation, aggressive paranoia, psychotic anxiety, reactive depression, and all the rest. Do you ever consider that I too feel exactly the same as you do, and if it were not for our ... ah what's the use of explaining it to you.   Forget it. Come on, let's go get a beer somewhere.

THE LIFE OF THE ARTIST IN MONTPARNASSE

The Bums have decided to become *artiste-peintres*, and so they go to Paris, rent an artist studio in Montparnasse, put on artist smocks and bérets, and to get started paint on the walls of their studio everything that is inside the room. It's a large square room with a high ceiling and one window looking onto the street. Working together in perfect harmony they first reproduce the window on the wall opposite the window, so that now there is a perfect replica of the window, so realistically done that one cannot tell which is the real window. Then they paint the paintings hanging on one wall, all of them self-portraits of the Bums artfully framed, so that now all the paintings of themselves also appear on the opposite wall, but flattened into that wall, and yet just as well done and as convincingly as the originals. In one corner of the room two desks are standing next to each other against the wall. They paint the desks, and the chairs in front of the desks, in the corner of the studio directly opposite the real desks and chairs. The composition and the perspective is so perfectly executed that if someone were to enter the room and decided to sit at one of the desks, that person could not possibly distinguish the real desks from their reproductions. On the ceiling they paint everything that stands on the floor, the working table, the stools, the paper basket, the easels (they each have their own easel), and themselves too, but upside down, of course, and yet so exactly replicated that someone standing on his or her head looking up at the ceiling could not possibly detect any difference between what is on the floor and what is painted on the ceiling. Eventually all the objects in the studio are mirrored on the walls and on the ceiling, including the easels in the center of the room with the large canvas propped on them representing the room and the two Bum-artists standing before their easels in the process of painting a portrait of themselves. They then paint themselves with a smile of satisfaction on their faces standing before the easels in the painting of the easels they have reproduced on the wall. Finally they paint themselves sitting at the imaginary desks, head between their hands, elbows resting on top of the desks. For a while they stare at themselves sitting at the imaginary desks, then walk to the real desks, sit down, place a large sheet of paper on the desks and begin to sketch a picture of themselves sitting at the desks sketching themselves.

TITLES

Though they will not admit it openly, the two bums often deplore the fact that they have not gained recognition for their achievements, and so they sometimes speculate as to what the title of a book about them would be if such a book were to be written. Over the years the bums have kept adding possible titles to the list they would propose to the potential chronicler of their twin-life if such a person were to offer his or her services.

Here is that list:

The Twilight of the Bums
A la Recherche des Bums Perdus
Bumlet & Julette
The Bumwake Celebration
Also Sprach die Bums
Among the Bums
Die Bümmerdämmerung
The Bum Rap
Waiting for the Bums
The Divine Bum Comedy
Journey to the End of Bumhood
Loose Shoes & Other Bum Stories
Long Talking Bad Conditions Bums
L'Education Sentimentale des Bums
Sorrisi a Bumsvilla
Eine Version Unsere Bumlebens
From Bumsville to Peoria
The Brothers Karabumzov

POETICS

The bums are discussing **the poetry of their existence** and arrive at the conclusion that the very fact of the **irreverence of their dual-beingness** destroys the solo solipsism of the poet who thinks he or she can find his or her voice, as the saying goes, by writing lyrical poetry, a romantic fallacy akin to the obligatory **starving-in-the-attic-tubercular-bleeding prerequisite for poetry.**

Indeed the two bums are aware that their **negligence of style** in everything they do, **their coldness** and especially **their superficiality,** and **their disdain** of the arrogant pomposity of lyrical poetry **is their forte,** and that their friendship is like a great poem, **because friendship tends to blur language, and generally gives rise to imprecise and fuzzy blubbering,** which is the essence of real poetry.

DAS LEBEN IST EINE COLLAGE

One day Displaced Person One, for no apparent reason, regressed into his native tongue and gesturing wildly said:

Ich wurde von meiner Mutter in einen Schrank geschubst, Aber ich glaube jeder Mensch hat das was ich eine Schrank-Erfahrung nenne. Ya, jede Mutter sagt zu ihrem Kind mal du gehst jetzt in dein Zimmer und da bleibst du. Manche Kinder sind gerne in ihrem Zimmer allein andere haben Angst davor. Der Schriftsteller ist jemand der sich in einen Schrank einschliesst. Ich wurde auf eine Art ja am leben erhalten weil meine Mutter mich in den Schrank schieb sie gab mir noch einen Roman, meine Mutter gab mir Arbeit für mein ganzes leben. Das ist ein sehr grosses Geschenk.

Displaced Person Two was astonished and said, also regressing into his native tongue: Parfois, tu sais mon vieux, je ne comprends pas du tout ce qui se passe dans ta tête. Moi je crois que tu es en train de perdre la boule.

CLARIFYING THE FACTS

whdya roiling dames the belles of lilly
the sea of apricot the kiss of water
the night of felix the tails of dog casso
be now and then moreorless our
surpoem our cake of teth spikes of
mothergrudging grind ground my papa
putees saving haiti again 1916 with
his horse troops papa doc in diapers
when my dad showed forthe for empire
ture ture and the fgld mord duberedetl
whoah how many miles a day on beans
and hay where'd you get that red tie
frank? you look good on the poster
do-boy oh oh I soaked in the fountain
oh feel oh fell oh fell dead fell linguini
xxx you see how must the text of part
I enact wld is the turmoil of language
envision this a huge piece for middle
bing to never do ah

LOVE GAMES

The two old boys staggering down a dark city street, punching each other giddily, slapping the faces of parking meters, kicking trash cans, shouting imprecations in the empty silent patient night.

They spent the evening at Madame Rilke's salon de refuse, tippling her brandy and chatting about the old times when they were regular paying full fare customers and visiting the peep-holes to view the girls at work.

And now, stumbling back to their hotel rooms (they are in the big city reading papers at the meetings of their respective professional conventions), they are shouting about what they have seen through the holes. They were especially moved by one young novice guided in her responsive words and gestures by a teleprompter inserted in the mirror above the bed:

> *tell him how much it hurts*
> *spank him hard once now*
> *stick your index finger up his ass*
> *lick the tip of his cock*

Neither old prof has acknowledged what we must: namely that they are discussing the girl from the point of view of their respective intellectual points of view as professional scholars.

Old Boy One states with a humanitarian tone that from an Existentialist perspective he felt the novice did extremely well considering her lack of experience, and that in fact, he himself, in his position as a mere voyeur, was aroused.

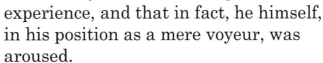

Old Boy Two argues deconstructively, from a post-structuralist position, that in his opinion, the chick was a total disaster, that her words and gestures were clumsy and ineffective, and that he cannot understand how in heaven any one can get *jouissance* from such a miserable performance.

COLONIAL HELMETS

One night, sleeping in the same bed in a cheap motel room (no need to specify where they were traveling to) the two bums dreamt the same dream at the same time. They dreamt that they were standing in the middle of a crowd of curious onlookers in front of which a series of executions were taking place, and this puzzled them, especially since everyone was wearing a colonial helmet with a chin strap, except them. The victims were being tortured and then decapitated. Suddenly one of the executioners and two helpers came towards the two bums, for it was their turn now.

The executioner asked: Which one of you wants to go first?

Without hesitation, they both replied in one voice, pointing to the other, He goes first.

Make up your mind, said the executioner obviously irritated, I can only decapitate one person at a time.

Suddenly, the two bums burst into laughter in the dream and embraced, for they remembered simultaneously that they had dreamt this dream before, and they knew that the images would be erased when they awoke. Still, a sense of betrayal lingered between them when they awoke.

WINTER WHEAT

One day, the bums [let's call them
the two old men for this occasion] went
out on a familiar walk. A good
mile through a stand of old oak,
down the steep cut to the sixty-
year old steel bridge, its rusting
structure suggesting a monument
to something [we know not what],
and thence northward along the
railroad tracks, in file, silently
[heads bowed, eyes to the ground] into
the fog collecting, rising.

Slowly along the winding deer
path downward toward the tracks
they went, each with a walking
stick [hand-carved, it should be noted, for
the sake of harmony], in file through
the dark woods, over the wet
compact of [dead] leaves, late in the
day, late in November [although it
could have been early December], the old
men trudging along.

The smaller, slighter of the two [and older perhaps by a couple of years] first,
leading, the larger one [larger not only in stature but also in imposture] following,
neither one a leader or a follower but rather taking up those positions
naturally, as, for instance, brothers might, although in that case a
competitive tension would be likely present [since brothers are usually more
inclined to be enemies than friends].

In old [tattered] overcoats, hats [that of the smaller one greenish, that of the larger
one brownish], and gloves [nondescript], carrying sticks fashioned rudely [by
hand, as already noted, probably with a pocket-knife] from windfall limbs, the old
men proceeded northward [in truth, more northeastward] along the ties, both
noting a band of green [the fog intensifying its green], a passing grain car had
obviously sown this field of winter wheat, now a healthy three inch stand,

thriving in the rock bed between the rails, and on the ties as well [if this notion can be maintained].

The one ahead stooped, pulled a few shoots out of the rocks, rubbed them between his fingers, then threw them down [correction: scattered them into the air].

What the old men were thinking cannot be revealed [how can it be? Stream of consciousness went out of business long ago]. It could be that they were thinking nothing, that the movement, the occasion, was occupying them completely [nothing is more real than nothing]. Their walk, then, could have been not unlike prayer [this is just a wild guess], a form of prayer, a rhythmic ritual muttering of ancient verses [yes, much better, ancient verses], verses collapsed into meaninglessness [excellent], meaningless and, therefore, valuable syllables.

But what they are thinking does not matter much, they are [the shift to the present tense here is deliberate for the sake of immediacy], after all, old men, out of the loop of generative illusion [nicely said], freed to exist plainly in a larger field [of winter wheat], their lives their own, for a while.

The old men walking along, ahead of them another bridge rising into the fogbank, and beyond it on a siding, a line of boxcars [digression: as he glances at the boxcars the smaller one recalls, for no specific reason, that in France, boxcars carry this inscription: 40 hommes ou 20 chevaux]. They pass the tail of a squirrel on a tie between the rails, a complete tail neatly severed at its base [this to point out that animals too like to indulge in railroad tracks]. Each man inspects the [loose] tail briefly with his stick, poking at it [it is dry, dead].

The slighter man, wiry, tough, picks up a stone from the railroad bed and hurls it at a rotting disconnected telegraph pole. The larger man comes alongside and fires his stone at the pole as well [it should be noted for the sake of accuracy that the smaller man throws with his left hand while the larger man throws with his right]. This contest continues until each man has hit the pole several times [neither man, however, can be declared the winner, for it was not a competition, just a little game].

Then they proceed, in file again, but this time the larger man ahead for a while, then dropping back, taking up the position in which he can keep himself organized, can keep himself from collapsing [although the larger one is younger, by a couple of years, as noted earlier, he is not in as good a physical condition as the smaller one who daily practices the art of Tai Chi], guiding himself by reference to the figure ahead [the more athletic figure], by the cold steel of the continuous rail, by the tender shoots of winter wheat.

To the man ahead have come a few words, not even a complete line, from a bitter poem, body words, shooting up, sudden pain from a deep muscle, **ineinander verkrallt** [it could be Trakl, but this cannot be ascertained]. The man pauses a second, half turns his head as if to check on the other old man. As he moves forward, the words form again, in his body [words are not always spoken aloud by the mouth], **ineinander verkrallt ... ineinander verkrallt ... ineinander verkrallt ...** echoing inside of him.

Near the middle of the second bridge over the stream, the old men take a piss [they do not remove their gloves to hold on to their cocks while pissing. It is a cold day].

Down through the dark stand of oak, following the deer trail, over the wet compacted dead leaves, the old men went. [Here the return to the past tense is deemed essential to disrupt the chronology and monotony of this winter walk in the winter wheat.] Down the cut by the bridge they went, and then northward [more or less] on a late November [okay, November it is] afternoon, into the lowering fog, into the obscured evening. Along the railroad track in single file they proceeded until, beyond the second bridge, they came upon a string of boxcars on a siding. [This encounter with the string of boxcars is so important that no intrusions will disrupt the rest of this paragraph, or for that matter the next two paragraphs.] These they began to inspect, peering into the doorway of each open car, examining each one carefully, as if they expected to find something there. Although, perhaps this gesture was merely the idle curiosity of old men who gaze without interest at whatever presents itself, at whatever lies before them.

One of the boxcars was made of wood, like the others dramatically spray-painted by disenfranchised youth in distant cities, magnificent, huge dayglo letters of the alphabet so artfully designed as to obscure their origin. Into this wooden boxcar the smaller of the two men jumped. Then he turned and reaching out to his friend he pulled him aboard.

Empty, walls and floor of heavily splintered wood. Both doors drawn open.

Empty, only a few strands of baling wire, flat bands of black steel. Sitting down, using each other's back for support, the men took up position. The one facing the west door, the other the east.

Here they sat in silence for a long time, for an unusually long time [intrusion: it is difficult to establish how long an unusually long time is]. Here they sat relaxed, quietly, not moving. Inwardly, as children sit in a kitchen near their mother -- with mother, as she prepares supper. Here they sat back to back [in silence, except for the sound of their breathing], the fog gathering, lowering, weaving through the boxcar, inhabiting the space with the old men.

On a rail nearby paused a red-tailed fox, one paw on the rail, the other hovering, as if feeling something, alert to the presence of the old men, its nostrils in attentive quiver, its big bushy tail tense, still.

By pure blind association, since from where he sat he could not possibly see the fox on the railroad track, a few words of a fable [he once knew by heart] surged in the smaller man's body: **Un vieux Renard, mais des plus fins ... Fut enfin au piège attrappé.**

The larger man must have felt in his body that something was speaking inside his friend. He did not say anything, but with his back he pressed a bit harder on his friend's back.

Before they jumped down to the railroad bed, the old men tried to decipher [their one communal act on that day, except for the deliberate pressure of the back of the one against the other], the remnants of words cut into the wood at one end of the boxcar. The closed curve of a **T** or perhaps an **E**, the angle of an **L** or a **B**. Strange how long they inspected these few bits of words cut into the wood, bits of letters, bits of exclamation. [No, there was no carving of a heart pierced by an arrow, only letters, remnants of words.] Standing at the wall [squinting] in the act of study, the old men inspected, much longer than by any compass seemed necessary.

Then the old men climbed out of the car and retraced their steps, back to the place where they had begun [up the hill], walking in file, as before, the fog steady, unchanged, the wind still, things much as they were [earlier, during the descent]. Along the green ribbon of winter wheat glowing between the rails, over the first bridge, then up the steeply cut embankment [the old men puffing a little now] to the deer path winding through some woods.

Then along this path, over the soft wet compacted [dead] leaves, and then, from the valley came the burgeoning blunt sound of diesel engines pulling a heavy load, diesel engines hard at work, that deep powerful throbbing strain of diesel engines [the old men could smell the burning diesel oil]. That first, then that, accompanied by the sound of rolling stock, of steel wheels on the steel tracks.

Impoverished ironies stretch endless as continuously forged steel rails back and forth, **hin und her**, back into time and through time to nothing and beyond that place to nothing more, and to here, here to this empty text [full of silence and intrusions], and then to more, forever **ineinander verkrallt ... enfin au piège attrappé.**

THIS & THAT

One summer day, the bums at their ease on a park bench, their grand-kids scooting about in the sandbox, on the monkey bars, the sun flooding down, they got to talking about their own parents.

Bum 2 enquired, How did your old man die?

Bum 1 answered, In bed, in extreme old age, shouting for his mother.

Ah, yes, yes, I remember now your telling me that, years ago, years ago. I forgot, said Bum 2.

What about your father, asked Bum 1, how did he go?

He was burned alive in a furnace, Bum 2 explained calmly. There are records of this.

Ah, yes, yes, I remember now your telling me this, years ago, years ago. I forgot, said Bum 1.

THE BEAUTY OF LONELINESS

Loneliness is a natural state, says Old Guy One, I believe in loneliness beyond life, when we feel lonely among our friends it is only a presentiment of our lonely future or an after-taste of our lonely past.

Quite right, replies Old Guy Two, and I would add that since everything except loneliness is parenthetical, a passing perturbation, then loneliness is security.

I'll go further than that, says Old Guy One, hell is a nightmare without loneliness, without calm, without consistency, therefore loneliness is our dream of paradise.

Yes, concludes Old Guy Two, too much distance or too much closeness is loneliness, that is the beauty of loneliness, and that is why loneliness is a natural state.

EXCHANGING GIFTS

As established earlier, the old boys share the same birthday (both born under the sign of Taurus, which means that they live on this planet with their feet on the ground and their heads in the clouds). And so on this special day in May, after having consulted their horoscope in the local rag, which required little interpretation on their part since it stated quite appropriately that, quote -- *Gift adds to wardrobe, you'll be pleased with body image, popularity will zoom upward, you'll cause people to laugh even through tears* -- the two old boys exchange gifts.

You open yours first, says Old Boy One, obviously pleased with his choice of a gift.

Old Boy Two holds in his hand the long narrow box neatly wrapped and pretends to be guessing what's inside. He's about to unknot the red ribbon when Old Boy One stops him.

Read the card first.

Old Boy Two opens the envelope, reads silently and explodes into laughter [hard to tell from here if the laughter is genuine].

Don't you think it's hilarious? asks Old Boy One.

Very funny, very funny, but I am not ready to give up sex for golf, says Old Boy Two, as he unwraps his gift. Oh what a gorgeous tie, he exclaims, exactly what I needed! He goes to the mirror and holds the tie against his chest. Perfect! And look at this fantastic design, it's a golf club!

Do you really like it, or you're just saying that? says Old Boy One with a look of uncertainty on his face. It's pure silk, you know.

I love it, I just love it, replies Old Boy Two, and it'll go well with my brown suit ... now you open yours.

At this point, no further description of the scene is necessary, for by pure coincidence, Old Boy One receives exactly the same card and the same gift he chose for his friend. But such coincidences are not unusual with people born on the same day, under the same sign.

THE CREATURES OF CULTURE

As demonstrated on several occasions in this collection, the two old guys are creatures of culture, and so on this special day, the day of their birth, they receive their presents from their respective wives, but without much excitement, for once again they expect yet another hardbound edition of Anna Karenina or a new recording of Malher's Fifth.

Old Guy One unwraps his gift first, and with a look of astonishment exclaims, Oh look! I got a massaging machine. And look, you don't even need to plug it in. It works on batteries.

Wow! says Two. Lemme see.

What did you get? asks One.

Two's fingers struggle to open his package, a rectangular box.

What is it? inquires One as he stares inside Two's box.

I'm not sure, replies Two puzzling over the contents of his box.

Looks like a toaster. Yes, that's what it is a toaster, explains One to his friend, as he lifts the object out of the box.

You're right, it is a toaster, can you imagine that? Amazing, you get a massaging machine and I get a toaster.

Makes sense to me first we massage each other, and then we toast ourselves. I tell you, those wives of ours really know what's best for us.

BIRTHDAY

Every May the bums gather to celebrate their nativity, which, as decreed by Fate, occurred on the same day.

They burn the accumulation of the year past and of its ashes make a bread, a bitter bread with ashy texture, which they consume ceremoniously, with all those gathered for the occasion, the bums sipping only white vinegar.

Soon thereafter the festivities collapse into normal human sounds of pain, jealousy, joy, hunger, laughter, recrimination, lust, despair, pleasure, snoozing, and the two old men are left alone at the table of honor, its white cloth flapping like a luffed sail in the late afternoon breeze.

The old men look at each other, something they do not often do. They look at each other a long time, as if to imprint the features of the other in the brainpan. They gaze at each other as the kids fall in the swimming pool and a helicopter passes overhead, and as the women come to clear the table. One of the old men raises his hand slightly, as if he intended to say something to the other, but he does not. Whatever the old men are doing is enough, and suffices unto this day. Another year consumed.

THE DEATH CERTIFICATE

The Two Old Farts are discussing their death -- who will inherit what?

Fart One says, I assume that when you die I'll get everything you own, all of it.

Fart Two replies, I suppose the same goes for me -- if you go first, all of yours will be mine.

Of course, adds Fart One, whoever dies first leaves everything to the other: golf clubs, fishing gear and poles, wading boots, rifles and shotguns, motor cars, the little black address book, the certificates of deposit, the ...

Say! interrupts Two, speaking of certificates of deposit, how will I know when you are dead?

Easy, One replies, his closed hand tracing the flat line of the horizon, I'll send you a death certificate.

Two receives this information unflinchingly and turns to gaze into his friend's dear face. I'll beat you to it, he says grinning.

Oh no, you won't, One cries out, I've always been first in everything we've done.

THE QUESTION

Dear reader: somewhere in this volume, probably in pages you have already consulted since the two bums have more of a past than a future, you will find a literary effort concerning the sociology of wifehood. Would you be so kind as to consult that effort and tell us who you think **Sophie** is?

With our typical arrogance, it never occurred to us that the lit. effort in question is loaded with ambiguity on this point. Is **Sophie** the mother, the mistress, or, indeed, the wife?

Please write to us and clear this up, if you would be so kind. We're in hot water until we hear from you. Answer with due caution, however, since no matter what your answer is, it will implicate you.

THE FIGHT

As it often happens in a lifelong partnership (even with old friends) the two bums had a fight. It started as a shouting match about something or other but quickly degenerated into ugly pushing, ugly shoving, and ultimately: violent fisticuffs.

You, dear reader, may wonder what caused such a tempest on the usually tranquil sea of their friendship ... [and wonder too at the excessive literary writing in the preceding two lines].

Even the two derelicts, when they reconciled and embraced after three weeks of refusing to exchange a single word could not recall the reason for this bitter dispute, but the black eye on Bum One and the swollen lip on Bum Two were proof enough of the violence of their combat.
[Such an enjambment, even in prose, as exampled above, was brought into the culture of poetry by Victor Hugo himself -- alas!].

You may, Dear Reader, if you wish, imagine a cause for this bloody fight, or, better yet, you may go sock your own beloved and crack his or her lip, bruise his or her eye, but as for us, we suspect that in the case of our two derelicts it was the same old reason that causes friendships to dissipate: **stubbornness!**

NIGHT BURIAL

As is often the case, indeed, if we may be so bold, as is always the singular case, it may be stated with indubitability that **Literature** (here we indict **Art** as well) refers, first and foremost, to itself; and, as a corollary to this first assertion, we asseverate that often it is **Literature** itself which is least aware of this fact.

If you have not yet given up the ghost in repellent boredom as yet, we offer as an example, before our own story begins, the Bartok/Shostakovitch/ Lehár number: B's parody of S unaware of S's parody of L. Are we boring you? On we rush.

It is night, deep night somewhere in Bohemia, and the bums, still hitch-hiking west toward the western foci of civilization and its discontents: Paris or Dachau. Deep night on a stretch of dark deserted road, the bums tossed out there by a busload of Irish Separatists Soccer Club members who mistook Bum 2 for an English lord, kicked them out after a good thrashing with their soccer shin guards. Deep night, the old bums exhausted, hungry, and so thirsty they are passing the business end of a tossed cigarette butt back and forth for the moisture in the tobacco. Rather than wait, they determine to set out on foot, to walk -- surely a town lies ahead, somewhere. The bums struggle along, side by side, hand in hand, lest they lose one another in the complete starless moonless night. Like the heroes of old, on this night, they have no private thoughts.

Perhaps, says one to the other, we are already dead. I was just about to utter that very thought, the other replies.

Soon thereafter the road tends downward and in a distance only defined by their appearance the old men could see a series of lights, perhaps torches, in a single file, moving slowly toward them. About two kilometers ahead, although calculating distance without reference points is -- oh well, this rhetoric already implies its conclusions so why waste time and space, eh?

The rest is quickly narrated. The old guys jump off the road and hide in a ditch. The string of lights draws nearer, now moaning is heard, formless moaning but moaning finding a form in that formlessness, moaning discovering a rhythm of sorts, a shape to contain the implied grief. At 50 meters a mule pulling a small cart is noted in the semi-darkness (for it is not as dark now as before because we have removed the clouds that were hiding the Moon -- eh! why not). On either side of the cart, torch bearers. Behind, a small group of hooded figures. Everyone moaning, moaning from the pit of the stomach, the way Tibetan Buddhist monks pray. At 20 meters a coffin is revealed atop the cart. Also, inflated rubber tires on the mule cart.

It's a night burial, whispers one to the other. Yes, whispers the other back, a big sinner. Only big sinners are buried at night.

Soon enough the burial procession has disappeared from sight and the old men are again on the road in the dark (the Moon is back behind the clouds), stumbling along, holding hands, now certain that a town lies within walkable distance.

One of the bums says to the world and his friend and himself, it doesn't get any better than this. One replies, my thought exactly, his brainpan working furiously to assemble the depressing realizable lyric which Edith Piaf planted there some 50 years ago.

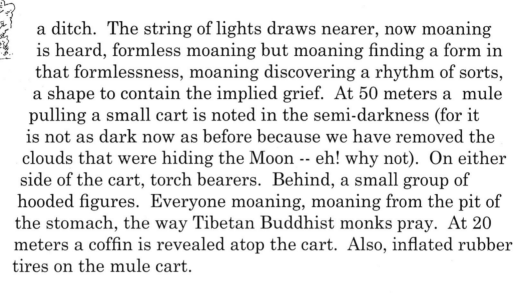

CERTIFICATION OF PURITY

We the undersigned members of the Cervantist Society wish to state for the record that your literary effort **NIGHT BURIAL** has been cleared of all charges brought before our body pertaining to elements in that effort thought to have been plagiarized from **DON QUIXOTE**.

A double-blind computer scan, the DNA testing of our profession, betrays no literary influence whatsoever in your piece.

We do wish to observe, however, that the Lehar operetta which Shostakovitch rakes over the coals so in the first movement of his 7th Symphony was the favorite tune of Adolph Hitler, especially in those glory days when the Reich was on the march southwest to its biggest prize: Paris. Thus, in mocking it with such violence, we hear Shostakovitch's intention to pound old Lehar down the Furher's throat.

Yours respectfully,

Ramón Hombre Della Pluma
President ex cathedra

THE PEAR

One quiet lazy fall day their black-market contacts all made, their pockets thick with yen and military scrip from various shady deals bargained and settled in the back alleys of Yokohama, the two draftees slipped into their zoot suits (custom made in Hong Kong) and jeeped off in an officer's vehicle to a famous tattoo parlor in the Tokyo Ginza.

Tattooing, as our readers are certainly aware, is something of an art form in Japan, although suffering some during the post-war occupation and reconstruction period, which eventually necessitated in most parlors the institution of a side business to thicken the cash flow, in this case the ever-reliable sex shop with all the essential instruments of pleasure.

So the **Big Good Time Sex & Tattoo Shop** was quite a busy power point, and there our two draftees wended their way to get laid and tattooed (young men, trust us, don't know which end is up).

Draftee One was first under the tattooing needle, the master creating a small pear on his right buttock. When One rolled aside to another table for his pear to cure a while, Draftee Two bared his back and prepared for an enpicturement of his first parachute jump in full battle gear, a big multicolor picture of the open chute stretching from shoulder to shoulder, but just as the master's needle was about to draw the first line, Draftee Two stood up, bowed to the master and paid for his and his friend's tattoo with an arrigato gozimus.

The master turned to slather curing cream on One's pear, humiliated that personal need did not allow him to refuse the cash for work he had not done. Probably only readers with any sense of history will have a clue as to why Draftee Two also felt disturbed, in an unexpressed way, on that special day, 40 years ago, when Draftee One got a pear needled into his ass, and he got nothing.

THE PRECIPICE OF HISTORY

Early in life the old guys were erased, wiped out from the blackboard of history, screwed free from the heart of motherland.

True. And so they spent their years trying to get back in, seeking nominal recognition, trying to write themselves into existence.

True. But no luck. The Kike and the Mick are mere statistics.

True. So what's all this belated clamor about the disposition of their remains?

Let their bodies and souls (if they have souls) vanish, vanish into the bottomless precipice of history.

HOLOCAUST THEME PARK

The two bums are bums of course but that doesn't mean they have not been exposed to certain approved elements of culture. Thus, for example, if you tested them with a grouping of pictures of buildings from the so-called **Chicago School** they could instantly discriminate a Sullivan from a Wright. Or give them a few bars of a sonata to listen to and they'll tell you without any hesitation if it's Beethoven or Westergaard. That's how cultivated they are. But so what?

Well, of course, **Kultur** doesn't matter much, it's what burns first, and fastest, when dictators take over.

Anyway, on this particular day the Bums find themselves at the new Holocaust Museum in DC, a few days after the final combustion in Waco.

They pay, receive their victim I.D. card, and move along with the crowd up and up to the top of the museum, **der dritte stock**, where the tour starts. They have barely looked at the first photographic display when Bum 1 draws his friend aside and faces him. Are you thinking what I am thinking? he asks.

Bum 2 replies, Guggenheim.

Exactly, nods One, Guggenheim.

2 takes 1 by the hand (old guys often hold hands) and together they rush out of this so-called museum. Down in the street in front of the building they are accosted by a group of protesters shouting: **Six million lies**.

The Bums join in. #1 shouting Guggenheim-Guggenheim. #2 chanting Disneyland-Disneyland. And both offering up the Nazi **seig heil**. The protesters form a circle around the two bums and begin shouting these strange words too, and saluting as well.

A FISH STORY

One day the two old geezers were fishing off the end of a decrepit boat dock, a new sport for these guys, used as they were in their younger years to power games such as tennis, ping-pong, racquetball, golf, wrestling, parachuting, mountain climbing.

Fishing is for the birds, said the Mick.

Yes, replied the Frog, fishing is for women.

And yet, they sat there on the rotting boards, each leaning on the piling between them.

Across the river and through the trees, said the Frog.

And a river runs through it, added the Mick.

And yet, the spring day was warm, blooming dog flowers lining the bank, and the river ran fast with spring run-off.

You know, said the Frog, I miss my mother.

Me too, said the Mick, I miss my mother, and my father.

Me too, said the Frog.

And so, on this quiet soft day early in spring, the fishing went on, the two friends held their poles faithfully, neither man minding the bait, or the hook, or the occasional tug on the line.

HOT TEA IN GLASSES WITH LEMON

This story the Yid told the Mick one evening as they sat at the dining room table in the Mick's house and reminisced after a rather copious meal.

It's late in the afternoon. The Gestapo will be up shortly. They'll sit with tante Rachel and the rest of the family at the dining room table drinking hot tea from tall glasses with slices of lemon floating in the tea, and they'll nibble little pieces of gâteau. Their uniforms will be black, neat and slick, with Gestapo symbols sewn on the sleeves. Their big black Mercedes-Benz will be parked in front of the house. After they finish the gâteau, they'll unbutton their jackets to show us their SS tattoos, then they'll pull their revolvers out of their black holsters, aim them at us and shoot. The half-empty glasses of tea will shimmer on the table before toppling over and the tea will get mixed with the blood of my family and drip from the table onto the oriental carpet. Me I will observe all this because I will be hiding under the dining room table, and that's why I can tell you this story now, my dear friend, because you see they didn't see me hiding under the table, picking up the crumbs of the gâteau.

The Mick listened closely as the Yid revealed this story. After a considerable period of silence, it was the Mick's turn to speak. He began: *It is late in the afternoon. The Gestapo will be up shortly ...*

DEUTSCH-LAND - DEUTSCH-LAND
GERM-ANY   GERM-ANY

Af-ter h-ear-ing the n-ews, the bums imme-dia-te-ly book-ed two seats one-way to Düssel-dorf. Tw-o s-eats one-way.

(Wh-en o-ne a-chi-eves a cer-tain a-ge [we don't spe-ci-fy] one is en-abl-ed to act w-ith true spon-ta-nei-ty.)

T-wo ti-ckets first-clas-s to D. O-ne-way.

The old bo-ys l-ike first cla-ss, the big con-so-le chairs, the end-less ser-vice, the pret-ty fli-ght at-ten-dant-s flit-ting a-bout them li-ke spar-rows, as if the old men had buck-ets of se-ed to br-oad-cast.

(H-ey, did you get a snif-f of lit. in the last pas-s-age? Wasn-t some-thin-g a lit-tle lift-ed a-bout it?)

The eld-er-lings en-joy the end-less suc-es-sion of fin-e wi-nes in first-class ac-com-mo-dat-ion, the re-al clo-th table-clo-ths and na-p-kins in fir-st clas-s, and esp-ecia-lly tha-t lyr-I-cal sens-e of lo-ss ol-d men fe-el in the pres-ence of wom-en of ju-ice.

(Ah, wo-men o-f ju-I-ce!)

The old buf-fs have not lo-st their brai-ns to-tall-y, ho-we-ver. The-y k-now en-ough to pur-po-se-ly le-ave the-ir seat-belts un-buck-led some-wha-t when the F-A's scur-ry to ad-monish them as 9-11 hea-vy rot-ates at max-i-mum thru-st, the boy-s de-cla-re them-sel-ves hel-p-le-ss to bu-ckl-e up, this is their first fli-gh-t, they only spe-a-k Far-see, and hel-p m-e fir-st the other gu-y is fak-ing it. Ah, the sc-ent of avail-a-ble wome-n, so deli-ci-ous-ly unset-tl-ing. A-h, i-t i-s al-most be-tt-er in reco-l-l-ec-tion.

Bum 2:   Spea-k for you-r-self, ass-hol-e.
Bum 1:   I kn-ew ther-e was to-o much hy-phe-na-tion in this stor-y.
Bum 2:   Shut-up.
Bum 1:   O-K.

O-ver the At-lant-ic non-stop, one-way, to Düs-sel-Dorf?

Wa-rum rei-sen die Penner-men-chen zum Düssel-Dorf zu-ruck?
       why tra-vel   bums   to   D   back?

We wi-sh the ta-le to achi-eve crui-sing spe-ed now, we sme-ll mu-le glu-e.

As you wi-sh. The bu-ms, stil-l a lit-tle tip-sy, from the fl-i-ght (you kn-ow
the ef-fects of al-cohol at 35-00-0 ft) have pre-sented them-sel-ves at the
sec-u-rity ga-te at the test-track of DM (Deutsch-land Mo-tors).

Go fas-ter.

O-K.

Theydemandtoseethedirectortheywanttobehiredasdummies
forthenewmodelcrashtests ...

N-o-t s-o f-a-s-t.
O-K.

I re-peat. They demand to see the director, they want to be hired ...

Hy-phe-na-te.

O-K. I con-ti-nue. As dum-mies for the new mo-del cra-sh test-s, what the x, if they can us-e fre-sh ca-da-vers (wi-th next-of-kin-permiss-ion, of co-ur-se) thin-k of the impro-ve-ment u-sing live sub-jects -- and be-sides, the bo-ys can use the ca-sh, you k-now wh-at it-s li-ke to li-ve on fi-x-ed in-come in time-s of infl-a-tion. An-d wh-o woul-d wan-t to mis-s a ch-an-ce to serv-e der Vater-land und das Deutsch-tum? And, ü-ber al-les, Sie ver-steh-en das the bet-ter the dum-my / the bet-ter the car. Nich-t w-har?

W-ow! To-o fast. What are you guys talking about?

Bum 1:   To-day's news, my fri-end.
Bum 2:   For on-ce, I can't impro-ve on tha-t.

You me-an you w-ant to do the Menge-le th-ing a-gain? (This is con-ta-g-ious.)

Bum 1:   A-gain? Tel-l me wh-en it sto-pped/stup-id.

Bum 2:   Z-war. Ca-ll u-s when it sto-ps.

But at lea-st Sie vil-l ha-ve the pro-te-c-tkeit of cra-sh helmuts, seat-rest-ungs und air-beutels. Alle-s kl-ar? Cer-tain-ly.

Bum 2:   Of cour-se. Be not over-dis-turb-ed.

Bum 1:   To be sure. Sch-laf-fen Sie who-l,
          mei-nen Kind-er.   s-leep   you   we-ll
               my   chil-dren.

SLOGANS

These are some of the slogans the two bums shouted during their revolutionary days:

Ah did they shout slogans against those who piously those who copiously those who critically those who tricolor those who bumper-sticker those who inaugurate those who hit you on the head those who believe they believe those who trucify & armisticize those who love it or leave it those who think they think those who croak croak & those who quack quack those who caca & pipi those who have feathers & panaches those who sing in tune those who mumble in their chin those who chew slowly sideways those who screw in the brains those who deliberate those who fuck in the dark those who spitshine those who eat too much those who close their eyes those who thumb their noses those who fix bayonet those who are too white those who never blush those who plug holes those who bury the living those who statue liberty those who float & never sink those who can you hear those who ask too many questions those who have all the answers those who club contusively those who dig graves for children those who fuck flies in the ass those who jerk off with gloves on those who never cry those who have their daily meals six times a day while others have their daily bread approximately once a week or less ...

... and this is only a partial list.

SOLO

Bum One is alone in his room sitting in a chair facing the wall talking to himself very softly.

I am observed to do pick at.
If ever I do drop a.
Shall we consider then in the.
It's the placenta of.
Or, failing, that I.
Her fruity breasts.
One more and for the.
To begin with, of course.
Her nipples with.
Kölnischeswasserbrand which.
My breathing stopped for.
Thus.
Well really you know and.
How can I bring my pear.
Even after every, without.
Words shall put forth for.
Too happy to.

Bum Two walks into the room. What are, asks he, here you yourself to again talking?

SHARED FAMILIARITY

I wonder if one particular aspect of what we share, of the movement you and I share, is an aspect of this phenomenon? asked Old Friend One. Namely that for long periods of time I literally lose the language -- for weeks, months, I stammer, I mumble, become absent from my own speech. Do you know what I mean? I cannot write even a simple letter to a friend, find a simple response to the dumbest question difficult to articulate. I growl all the time at my dog, my cat, my lovely daughter. Growl at my poor wife for asking the most innocent questions: **Why are you saving this empty shoe box in your closet?** And I bark at her: **Don't touch it! I need it for something**, though I have forgotten what that something was. Shout at her when she suggests, oh so gently, trying to drag me out of the house: **How about a movie this afternoon?** And me I grumble: **Bah, what's the point, there's nothing good playing, it's all crap these days!** If I do manage a few miserable words they are apt to be received language: **What time is it? What's for dinner? What's on TV?** Months go by before I begin to feel the return of words. Very strange. I wonder if it is at all familiar to you too, this phenomenon? I suspect it is.

Damn right it is, Old Friend two replied.

QUESTIONING THE WOMAN OF GREAT RESISTANCE

Gentlemen:

*Concerning **The Woman of Great Resistance** what do you mean by **great resistance**? Does it mean that the lady is strong, robust, tall, muscular, that she can endure the worst, that she is hard as nails? And when you say that it was a **gloomy day**, should one understand that it was raining that day, or snowing, or thundering, I mean, you could have been more specific, after all it was an important day for history?*

*I do not wish to sound too nit-picky, but in the second paragraph (if one can call paragraphs those curious blocks of words in which you enclose your meaning) does **nameless** mean that the two protagonists in question do not have a name, or have forgotten it, or do not wish to reveal it, or else shall one assume from the deliberate vagueness implied here that the authors are afraid to reveal the names of those two poor souls who are about to be extinguished?*

*And that's not all. No, that's not all. In the same paragraph, **thieving trash-hackers fucking worthless**, do you really think it is necessary to accumulate adjectives to such a degree in order to indicate the character of the two bums? Wouldn't one or two of these adjectives suffice? After all the situation in which the two bums find themselves calls for a touch of restraint and decorum.*

*I hope you do not find these comments impertinent, and that you will accept my questioning of this piece as a gesture of genuine interest in your work. Speaking of which, in the next paragraph, I get the sense of **olive trees**, it's obvious, but frankly I cannot make heads or tails of what you are trying to suggest with **skulls**.*

Need I go on? It's a pity that you could not control your language, you are working with such a splendid subject, and it gets worse on the second page. There the ambiguities are so flagrant that, to tell you the truth Gentlemen, I had great difficulty forcing myself to read on to the end of the piece, though I must admit that the final two lines moved me to quiet reflection.

> ***Do not despair, one of the thieves was saved***
> ***Do not presume, one of the thieves was fucked***

There is a certain something in these lines in spite of the obscene last word, a kind of roundness, a symmetry of syntax, an equality of terms which I personally greatly appreciated.

Well, I hope these few critical remarks will be accepted with grace. I could not prevent myself from expressing them.

Yours truly

The above letter was received by the authors of THE TWILIGHT OF THE BUMS on October 1st of this year. It was not signed, and no return address given on the envelope, although we suspect from the handwriting (yes the letter was handwritten with lots of elegant swirls) that a woman wrote it. We are reproducing it here *verbatim*, that is to say exactly like the original. The words in **bold** are, of course, from THE WOMAN OF GREAT RESISTANCE which can be found on page 29 of this volume. We feel that it is important for us to make our readers aware of such goings-on.

DEAR READERS

Somewhere in this collection
you will find or have already
found **Holocaust Theme Park**
and you are perhaps as disturbed
by it as we are, perhaps even shocked.

But know that the old bums are too.

Know that after the pathetic carnavalesque
demonstration in front of the museum
they went back to their seedy hotel room
and sat there long into the night
in humiliated silence, passing
a big green bottle of *Thunderbird*
back and forth.

[Here we break off the poem mode and shift to mother prose, the figure which the Muse always invokes when she is in trouble]. First, dear readers, know that the bums are not about to present their credentials, their bona fides as it were, to speak about this matter. After much passing of the *Bird* what became clear to the bums was that it takes more than a museum to create **one weasel of tear** for the memory of the humiliated and slaughtered millions who have met their Fate, and even for those who are still alive to forestall that eventuality, although the bums are not sanguine about that. And so, from their point of view, the only memorial suitable, the only Museum of the Holocaust, is the evening news on television, any network will be just fine, preferably in color, although black and white will do just fine as well. The strong cheap wine did not allay the angry bitterness of the old men, nor should that have been expected.

AT THE BARBER SHOP

Once a month the boys go for a trim and a shave,
each time to a new place (men love variety, as we all
know). Once a month they defy fate and order the
barber to trim what's left on the head and shave the
face, a more reliable source of hirsutity. The boys
like this for several reasons. First, it is something
to do. They need a reason to get out of the house,
to get out of the wives' hair. Second, they get
to refresh their map-reading skills (an important
military attainment), and also to read the latest
issue of **Sports Illustrated**. Third, they like to
create a little scene when they happen upon open,
no-appointment shops. When the barber says,
Next! the boys go into their *before you, Gascoigne*,
number, with its various phrases -- *age before
beauty, horse before cart, spoon before soup*, and
so on. Fourth, there is the possibility of getting a
shave and trim by a lovely young lady barber who
usually wears nothing at all under her white barber
smock and whose unencumbered breasts sometimes
rub inadvertently against the boys as she leans over
to trim the sideburns. Fifth there is barber shop
talk. Sixth the telling of the jokes -- *did you hear
the one about*, etc. Seventh, the sound of barbering
-- the snip of the scissors, the hum of the hair dryer,
the scrape of the straight razor, the brief groan of
the hot lather machine, the whip of the fan blade
overhead, the sexy chat of the barbers as they work,
the banter, the billingsgate. Eighth, the fall of the
hair, the hair on the apron, the hair on the floor,
the mundos of hair, the barber's brush brushing
the hair off the boys' shoulders. Ninth, the mirror
held behind the head. Ten, the hot towel on the
face. Eleven, the slap and scent of the cologne as it
is applied (especially by feminine hands). Twelve,
the pull of the comb through the hair. Thirteen,
we almost forgot, the too hot and then slightly too

cold water of the shampooing. Fourteen, the last
touches and twitterings of the scissors. Fifteen,
the snap of the apron as the barber helps one out of
the chair. Sixteen, the tip after the assessment of
the quality of the work and the exactly appropriate
amount of the tip. What have we forgotten? Ah
yes, the delicious way that one drifts free of oneself
and one's concerns as the barber performs his or her
ministrations, yes, great ease, ease and travel, and
as in all life, the wish for it to continue, to go on, just
for a little while more, a bit more, precisely now as it
is ending, how one wants more, no matter how little,
down to a hair. Seventeen, the bus trip to the real
Chicago hot-dog stand. Eighteen, the proprioceptive
experience in the lurching bus, the boys banging into
each other and other passengers. And, oh yes, how
could we have forgotten the shoeshine performed at
the same time as the haircut, not to mention the
possibility of a manicure.

A BIT OF HISTORY

Our two friends first met in a hastily trenched shallow foxhole in Yongdong-po as Chesty Puller's men crossed the Han River and drove into the capital at Seoul.

No, that's a form of the truth, but not the exact historical fact.

The bums met when Bum Two flew over to Tachikawa from Kimpo in a C-47 and traded his load of cigarette cartons, all Camels, for several cases of Old Kentucky Waka Bum One had traded for bootleg film.

This is closer, a form of the truth to be sure, but still lacking the actual ingredient of verifiable facts (lots of historical events are of dubious credibility).

Perhaps they met at an R&R resort in Kobe, that sounds almost right. One would have jeeped down from Yokohama and maybe Two would have flown over from Kimpo, maybe ...

The real truth, however, but please keep it to yourselves, is that our two bums met one summer night in a house of pleasure in Shimbashi, sharing the same bottle of booze, the same room, and the same girl. The booze was Old Kentucky Bourbon, the room bare and nondescript, the girl said her name was Sumikosan, that she would love them both equally forever and ever.

Ahso deska.

DUEL AT SEA

♦

The
Old guys
Are out on
The bay fishing
In one of their grand-
Son's flatboats, a modest
Unstable affair with a two
Horse-power trolling motor and
A pair of collapsible oars in the bow.
It is their birthday and they are not feeling
Too happy about that -- the years are adding up
And the old guys have enough reasons to be taking
Them seriously, to feel the sad toll of the bell vibrating
Through their bones in that special twofold way that bells
Vibrate, as the poet himself told: Erst in dem Doppelbereich
Werden die Stimmen ewig und mild sein. Poets are so perceptive.
Sea bass is the catch they are after today -- the famous trophy fish
On the endangered list and thus dangerous to the boys too (boys is
What they are beginning to be called. A very depressing sign, indeed).
Anyway (it is hard not to digress when telling a fish story), the old guys
Are not feeling well at all, they are feeling old: the government is sending
Them forms, burial societies want to stop by for a chat, Sears has sent them its
Mature Wisdom catalog of prosthetic appliances, canes, crutches, handles for the bathtub,
Magnifying-glasses, inflatable rings for the toilet seat, ice-packs for sore body parts, aspirin.

♦   ♦   ♦   ♦

Anyway, heck, the ocean this late afternoon is especially dark, almost black, even though a full May sun is upon
it. From the west, the boys hear the sound of a fast approaching power boat, one of those superfast cigarette
jobbies drug runners use. The glare is such they cannot see it and they commence to worry some, thinking
the speeding boat might run them down. The danger implicit in this moment cheers the old guys up.
Just then the power boat comes into view, a bevy of lovely women on its bow, who, when they see
the old fishers, take off their bikinis and toss them into the water to give the boys a visual treat.
Damn, damn. Then they are gone, like all visions of loveliness, zerfliest wie Eitelschaum,
disappeared in a foamy frothy wake that looks like whale sperm (to some viewers).
Gosh, what a story. The old guys are standing up, screaming at the cigarette
boat to turn back, they are all excited, their flatboat, now surrounded on
all sides by the empty bikinis that look like deflated balloons, is
shipping water, wobbling. # One starts to giggle and
tickles his friend,who starts giggling and tickling
him back. Then, it seems from the distance,
as we recede to the safety of the shore,
that the two old guys are dueling
with their fishing poles,
can this be? Do you
see what we see?

THE FAILURE OF WORDS

By [k]now it **be** , to our   eaders, that two   old,   **are**
crea ures,   or,   Ffo
to   it luntly,   tha are   .   ?
But o/ne shoul nt   thi tha   **believe**   F
in the   of   . Our   old   re   aware
      tat are   get us   where   **want**   & prevnt there.
In fact, **is**   one exlained   why   ? always
      ma nage s   ing   yet   [*in italics*]   to

ho   !
Wht the   say   **cannot**   compltely,   one   not
mean at   (e   )
but one can   enouf to know   **not** cannot be.   Di yo
my   ?
Yes, I tink   what **you** ,   or not .   **Maybe**

A NOTE ON "DUEL AT SEA"

Those bits of cloth in the water, those bikinis floating in the surf like deflated balloons, in the context of the situation, have symbolic content complicated and yet somehow clearly decipherable.

It is easy to understand that sex has sped away on the cigarette power boat and left the old geezers in its wake futilely dueling, violence being the only thing left to them.

As such the old geezers may have stumbled into a great poetic moment if not a great poem.

NUMEROLOGY

Bum1:   22.

Bum2:   Ha ha ha. 44.

Bum1:   73.

Bum2:   Seventy what?

Bum1:   3.

Bum2:   Oh, that's a good one. 303.

Bum1:   Ah, what a beginning, 324.

Bum2:   Yes, yes, of course. But derivative. 9.

Bum1:   9? Are you aware that the 9 always cancels itself?

Bum2:   Yes, of course. But I'll stick with my 9.

Bum1:   It sobers one up. How can I go on?

Bum2:   Start all over again.

Bum1:   Okay. 63.

Bum2:   Oh, oh, 63 ... 63. Yes, that one.

Bum1:   No, no good. 6 & 3 add up to 9.

Bum2:   We're stuck then. We've canceled ourselves again.

Bum1:   That's right. End of the game.

NEW YEAR'S RESOLUTIONS

It's New Year's Eve. No need to specify which year is coming to an end
and which will begin at midnight, that is unimportant, what counts is that
the bums are preparing (without even consulting each other) their lists of
New Year's resolutions.

Bum One's list reads as follows:

No more Baked Alaska
No more Beef Wellington
No more Chocolate Dredge Strawberries
No more Three Dip Banana Split with Hot Fudge
No more Ice Cream Sundae with Extra Nuts & Cherry
No more Bourbon
No more Bonbon

Bum Two's list reads this way:

No more wishing I were in Paris
Ah Paris Paris
drinking a bottle of Perrier
Ah Paris Paris
smoking Gauloises
Ah Paris Paris
sitting at the terrace of a café
Ah Paris Paris
on the Champs Elysées
Ah Paree Paree

THE BUMS WHO WOULD BE KINGS

The bums have decided that before they change tense, before they enter the void of non-being, they would like to experience one last great adventure -- to go out into the world and gain ultimate power, if not total omnipotence.

And so Bum One proclaims that for him the great adventure would be to sit on the Papal Throne in the Vatican and rule over the millions and millions of Catholics in the world.

Bum Two bursts into laughter, I can't believe this, you would be willing to give up sex, or even sex fantasies, just to be Pope? You're kidding.

You have a point there, says Bum One, forget the Pope.

I have already, says Bum Two still laughing.

What about you, what would you like to be? asks Bum One.

A king, I would like to be a king, replies Bum Two. An emperor even, a conqueror like Alexander the Great. Yes, I would like to be as powerful, as omnipotent, as Alexander the Great who conquered all of Capristan and there married the beautiful Roxanne and accumulated so much gold and precious stones that when he decided to return to his homeland because he was homesick and wanted to see his mama, he could only carry with him 0.5% of that rich stuff. Yes, I would like to conquer an empire.

I'll go with you! exclaims Bum One, and maybe along the way I too can conquer a little kingdom for myself. Come on, let's get started immediately. On to Capristan!

Dear Readers, we are sorry not to be able to report at this time the progress of our two bums. Since they set out for their great adventure, more than three months ago, we have not received any communications from them. But rest assured that as soon as we hear from them, we will report to you as faithfully as we can all the details of their great adventure. Meanwhile, if you don't mind, continue to do whatever you do when you are not listening to us.

A STORY ABOUT A STORY WITHIN A STORY

One day (here we go again dear readers) Bum Two (whomever) was telling Bum One a story `my life began` and for some unusual reason the latter `among empty skins` was actually listening ... a very unusual thing indeed, actually listening to the story `and dusty hats` that Two was narrating. Actively listening rather than interrupting, laughing, kibitzing, stopping, turning away `while sucking pieces of stolen sugar` eating a cold waffle, and in general co-creating intersubjectively the community language experience `outside the moon` of the narrativity. It was, to be sure, `tiptoed across the roof`, not much of a story. Indeed, and in fact, if you asked Bum One about it now ... a mere few hours after the telling `to denounce the beginning of my excessiveness`, he would in all likelihood not be able to recover a shred of it, nary a syllable would have survived the telling ... although `but I slipped on the twelfth step`, to be sure, he may in this disremembering be exhibiting rather more of a short-term aphasia `and fell`, an age-appropriate disability, than creating an interpretation of the text. (Hey, this is muddy stuff `and all the doors`, eh readers, bet you wish you had a tissue, and some soap.) We mean here, `opened dumb eyes`, meaning no disrespect to Bum Two, that the story was lost on Bum One not because of its innocuousness and banality, but because `to stare at my nakedness` the old guy's motherboard is cracked. (What?)

Anyway (you see here how the elderly love to get lost in anything, `as I ran beneath the indifferent sky`, in a city, in a mall and, as here, in a text), Bum Two went on `clutching a filthy package of fear` with his story, a story, which we can now reveal had one distinct and curious feature ... we'll say it plain:

It began in the narrator's adopted language, but soon enough, `dans mes mains` was flowing in the mother tongue of the narrator, a language which he hasn't spoken all that much these last 45 years, although it should be noted that in the course of his narration Bum Two often switched back `a yellow star` to his adopted language and at times even spoke both languages `tomba du sky and frappa my breast` simultaneously.

The story itself, as we say, was perhaps eminently forgettable, a tale of survival, of defeat and victory, a tale of heroism and villainy `et tous les yeux turned away in shame`, a tale of noble wanderings, of sadly proportioned departures and returns, mixed with grand scenes of powerful recognition ...
      `then they grabbed me ···` You wonder what's coming next, don't you dear readers? We do too `and locked me dans une boîte`. We're getting worried for the old guys, perhaps they'll even forget this story they are supposedly narrating.

But this, as we say, is pure conjecture. What elements composed the actual story `dragged me` are lost to us, as we have asserted. We press on `cent fois`. But before we do, let us pause here a moment to re-establish the narrative, to summarize `my life began in a closet among`, to draw in a last big breath `merde alors si on se répète`. The two old guys are sitting dry-assed (you like this locution we bet, `over the earth in metaphorical disgrace`, we bet this is likely to be all you can recollect of this tale, so far) on a pre-formed (to whose shape?) plastic park bench ... `tiens un banc! Qu'est-ce que ce banc peut bien foutre ici?` ... supplied by a local undertaker featuring this week a discount for double interments in their spanking new columbarium `while`

they threw stones at each other and burned all the stars
in a giant furnace.

One elderling is telling the other a story which for some unusual reason
the latter is actually listening to et les voilà tous exterminés
les pauvres diables attentively, without interruption. The story is a
literary masterpiece, we think, but it is lost to memory. All that remains
every day they came is the knowledge that the tale began in English
and soon transformed to French, and even Frenglish, pour mettre
leurs doigts in my mouth et aussi dans mon cul, even though
the content of the tale had a Greek flavor with a touch of Yiddishkeit in it,
a tinge of the Aegean and the Middle-Eastern.

(Forgive us, we enjoy so these elaborations, these asides, these excursions
and incursions. We are former military persons, which is no doubt
culpable here) ... and paint me black and blue.

Soon then, soon enough mais à travers un trou, the narrator either
brought his tale to its conclusion or was incapable of drawing more breath
to sustain the story, or, I saw a tree the shape of a feuille,
having throughout the telling experienced no encouraging response from
his audience -- much as a preacher will call out for a witness, and one
morning a bird flew into my head, will gather fuel for the telling,
can we get a witness here? Ah tu parles machin, ils sont tous
morts les témoins, for the final hooping solution transcendence,
lost his confidence, ran out of gas -- can we get a witness too? -- and ended
the story, all in one breath ...
        I loved that bird so much that while my blue-eyed
master looked at the sun and was blind I opened the cage
and hid my heart dans une plume jaune ... Bum One slid out a bit
on the bench, the better to turn to his friend, the better to look at him. He

was thoughtful, puzzled.

You know, he said, I have never heard that story before. Not in all the years of our friendship.

Bum Two, now reverted to his step-tongue, did not seem surprised. Obviously not. I just made it up on the spot, he said, from approved material of course, but newly composed for this occasion.

Hmm, replied One, that much I suspected. I was not questioning the tale itself, but the telling of it. Are you aware that during the telling you began in one language and ended in another, and that in fact at one point you even mixed both languages and spoke them simultaneously?

Really? I did that, I mixed Yiddish with Ladino?

Well, I don't know if it was Yiddish or Ladino or Javanese, but some of what I heard did have a Yiddish beat with a touch of music from Ukraine, but that was only the vehicle. What I heard, what I really heard was ghosts, the voices of the dead.

Hey, you OK boy? asked Two, this bench making you morbid?

I'm telling you, I heard, Bum One went on, the voices of the dead, the dead who have no story of their own to tell. They are here with us now. Hey this is too much, said Bum Two turning away from his friend, shaking his head in refusal, this is too much.

And there they left the story, and we leave them, two old dry-assed bums, sitting next to each other on a bench in the park. Now you know why we experienced such resistance as we attempted to tell this story of a story within a story. We beg your indulgence.

PLAYING THE NUMBERS

Every Saturday morning the bums go to the nearby drugstore to buy lottery tickets. They have been doing this since the first day the lottery became legal in the state where they live, and they will probably continue to do so until they win the big one or until they die or until the lottery becomes illegal (whichever comes first), even though they have never won anything.

They each buy one ticket, always playing the same six numbers. Bum One's numbers are: 5, 15, 19, 28, 42, 47; Bum Two's: 3, 7, 12, 27, 43, 54. Neither of them knows the secret meaning of the other's numbers, and neither has ever asked the other (even though they have bummed together for more years than even they can remember) to reveal that secret, though each has, of course, speculated about their possible meaning.

In the privacy of his mind Bum Two thinks that Bum One's 5 designates the month in which his friend was born, the 15 the day of that month, the 19 and the 28 the year of his birth, the 42 a year of traumatic consequences for his friend, and the 47 a year of great change in his life.

Similarly, Bum One has speculated that the 2 in his friend's set of numbers refers to the two wives Bum Two has had, the 7 to the number of children Bum Two has had with both wives, 12 the number of years he was married to the first wife, 27 the total number of years Bum Two has been married to both wives, 43 the number of times he has been unfaithful to both wives (though Bum One is not certain of this one), and 54 the number of years Bum Two has lived in the same place with or without a wife.

A DOZEN BUMSAYINGS

[words of comfort, consolation & advice]

1. If someone offers you the back of his or her hand -- take it.
2. To ease the burden during those times of enforced solitude which every human being must endure, repeat this saying three times: **Solo, como el Esparrago**. Be mindful, as you chant this saying of solitude, that while the asparagus spear grows alone, the whole field is shimmering in a lovely bluish late spring haze.
3. Wisdom tells us that it is better to determine gender after rather than before.
4. The correct response to trouble is gratitude.
5. Give until it hurts. (This one is much better in any language other than American).
6. To decompose is to live, too (here the comma makes the difference).
7. Always keep your back to the wall.
8. Man is neither angel nor beast, but when Man tries to be an angel he turns into a beast. [For further elucidation on this one please see ANGELS in this collection.]
9. Arbeit macht frei. (Only in this language does this saying make a kind of sense.)
10. The source of the trouble is not in the trouble, just as the key to the treasure is not the treasure. (Whoever said that is full of shit.)
11. We leave home in joy and return in sadness. (The Bums are not entirely responsible for this one.)
12. If you have a (   ), be glad. If you don't have a (   ), not to worry. Soon, a (   ) will be yours too.

THE LIAR

Bum One is telling his friend with all the
appropriate gestures and facial expressions the
heroic feats he performed when he
was in the war -- the big war.

Bum Two stops his friend and
says: You are lying to me.
You never did those things.

Bum One is clearly irritated
by the interruption: I know,
I know, but hear me out
anyway.

MICTURITION

We are told that old men confronting their mortality often replay mentally (or even in writing) the great moments of their lives, or they make lists of the things that have given them particular pleasure, for instance, making love, eating gourmet food, tasting expensive French wines, parachuting out of airplanes, reading a good book (especially if it is one they have written themselves), listening to music (classical, jazz, gospel, hip hop, opera, delta blues, heavy metal), having their backs scratched, getting a full body massage, shooting a subpar golf game, sleeping late, playing cards with the grandchildren and of course winning, gazing with the remnants of desire at the gorgeous bodies of the wives of their sons, permitting themselves the wish of outliving their enemies (and even their friends -- if the truth can be told), und so weiter.

We are also told that sometimes old men (though lately more and more women too) confronting their mortality seriously for the first time consider performing one final act, something preposterous they have always wanted to do but never had the courage for.

And so, one day Bum One asks Bum Two (no need to identify which is which, old age being a generic condition): Before you die, what would you like to do that you have never done?

To this Bum Two replies, without so much as reflecting for even a moment: I would like to walk bareass on the Champs Elysées and micturate in public, right in front of the people sitting at a sidewalk café. Bum Two pauses, his face fractured into what could have been interpreted as a smile, and then he asks his friend: And you?

The friend shrugs his shoulders indicating what can be interpreted as indecision, or it could be that he is moved in a special way by his friend's last wish, the one wish he knows his friend will never be granted. Then he sits down, he sits down on the curb of Storkwinkelstrasse, right there in Berlin, the city with no history to speak of.

Bum Two looks concerned too. This wish of mine, he says cautiously, sitting down in the gutter beside his friend, has grieved you, has hurt you. I am so sorry. I had no wish to insult you, at least not today.

Bum One remains silent for awhile and then, looking across the broad street at the imposing Bauhaus facades, he says: It is a beautiful wish, I know what you mean. You wish to turn back the clock to that Sunday morning in July, 1942. Your mama has sent you to the bakery and you are coming back to your apartment with a big loaf of bread, almost as long as you are. As you mount the stairs to the third floor you can hear your sisters laughing (or are they whining?) as your mother shouts something at your father, that good-for-nothing bum who will never amount to anything, and you are climbing a bit faster so as not to miss the excitement.

Bum Two hugs his friend and says: You got all this from a simple leak, a leak I haven't taken yet.

Bum One looks at his friend. They cannot ask more of you, he says, but they do.

Bum Two lifted his old friend up. Come on, he said, digging in his pocket for his traveler's checks, let's go to Ka-De-Ve and buy something expensive for our wives.

FELO DE SE

The bums have decided to commit suicide. They have reached an existential cul-de-sac. They are fed up with life. Bored silly. There is nothing left for them to do in this world. They have done it all: traveled in all the continents (including both the North and South Poles), made love to hundreds of beautiful women of all races (including their own wives, of course), written books (some published, though most of these out of print now, and some unpublished, but that doesn't matter), parachuted out of airplanes, climbed the highest mountains on this planet, fought wars overseas, gambled in the swankiest casinos of Europe, yes they've done it all, and now they are bored, fed up with life. Even the thrill of receiving their monthly Social Security checks has faded away. This is it. They want out.

You understand, the bums are experienced in suicides -- well, suicides manqués. We know of at least four attempts on their part which resulted in failed acts of felo-de-se. But this time the bums are serious. They will not fail. They have made a suicide pact to go together, and have even written the suicide note on a large piece of cardboard -- two words that say it all: **we apologize**.

In order to determine who would go first they flipped a coin. Bum One won (or should we say, lost?). The old guys decided on this procedure so that at least the death of one of them could be verified by the other, which means, of course, that Bum Two's death will remain unverified until his body is discovered next to his friend's.

And now it is time to act. Bum One is ready to swallow the poison (poison is what has been chosen after other modes of self-destruction were rejected because they are usually too messy) mixed with red wine in a finely etched crystal glass (for this special occasion the bums have selected a 1959 Morgon Grand Cru -- the bums are great connoisseurs of wines) when suddenly his hand hesitates as the glass approaches his mouth. Hey, say, he tells his friend, how do I know that once I have drank this stuff and died you will do the same?

Good question, answers Bum Two, very good question. As you know, I've been inclined to be a coward on many occasions.

Bum One sets the glass down on the table, rubs his chin with his hand for a moment, and then says: Look, why don't we think of a more equitable way of doing this?

Fine with me, replies Bum Two.

And so once again the bums have postponed their death. In fact, after having discussed the matter at length, they reach the conclusion that to put an end to one's life is a form of delusion -- for to leave one's life, one's works unfinished implies the possibility of success -- what is left unlived, untold, may contain the potential truth one always seeks -- those who kill themselves do so with the conviction that they would have reached that truth eventually had they lived to the proper end -- they die in the illusion of hope which in a way keeps the rest of us alive.

FINAL SETTLEMENT

The bums reflect:

It is important never to forget the mud-pile in which humanity wallows in pain.

The bums further reflect:

Having entered the era of multiple madnesses, pressed together like the folds of an accordion, humanity is rediscovering the boredom of repetition at the beginning of eternal return.

The bums shake their heads:

Humanity is suffering of the sickness of being because life is but a convulsive xerox copy of death. One tries to cure that by pretending to sooth mankind of beingness, and life of deadness, but nothing is more boring than health.

The bums shrug their shoulders:

The Divine Comedy of life can no longer be written as a future projection of the final collective settlement of accounts.

The bums sit down and put their heads between their hands:

Traveling without destination in endless round trips towards and away from something that has nothing more to do with life, humanity spreads everywhere its paleo-biological anguish.

The bums begin to cry:

This endless bleeding of life into death gives the appearance of life but in fact it is already death.

The bums throw themselves on the floor:

It is just a matter of deploying as much skepticism as possible as humanity oscillates between life and death.

The bums get up and wipe their eyes:

It is not an evolution towards a cure but towards more sickness and pain.

The bums throw their arms up in the air:

Sick humanity must force itself to enter into the repetition of its incurable sickness not by asking for final judgment at the end of civilization but by accepting the end of civilization.

The bums bang their heads against the wall:

The final judgment takes place in permanence in the simulation of non-judgment in neutrality, that is why it is called corruption.

The bums scratch at the wall with their fingernails:

The necessity of postulating the Apocalypse is already the Apocalypse because this postulation goes on forever.

The bums conclude sadly:

The time of settlement is here and now, we are all living-dead separated from each other only by the little plot reserved for us in the great cemetery of the universe.

The bums burst into laughter.

TWO BUMS LAUGHING

!! !! !! !! !! !! !! !! !! !! !! !! !! !! !! !! !!
!! !! !! !! !! !! !! !! !! !! !! !! !! !! !! !! !!
Ω Ω Ω Ω Ω Ω Ω Ω Ω Ω Ω Ω Ω Ω Ω Ω Ω
!! !!
Bum One: hahahahahahahahahaha
Bum One: hahahahahahahahahaha
Bum One: hahahahahahahahahaha
Bum One: hahahahaha**hahahahah**
Bum One: hahahahaha**h** *oho*
Bum One: hahahahaha**hahahah**
Bum One: hahahahahahahahahahah
Bum One: hahahahahahahahahahahah
Bum One: hahahahahahahahahahahahah
Bum One: hahahahahahahahahahahahahahh
Bum One: hahahahahahahahahahahahahahahah
Bum One: hahahahahahahahahahahahahahahahah
Bum One: hahahahahahaahaahahahaha
Bum One: hahahahahahaha**hahahahaha**
Bum One: hahahahahahahah _{aaaaaa}
Bum One: hahahahahahahah ^{aaaaaa}
Bum One: hahahahahahaha**hahahahaha**
Bum One: hahahahahahahahahahahaha
Bum One: hahahahahahahahahahahah
Bum One: hahahahahahahahahaha
Bum One: hahahahah
Bum One: hahahahah
Bum One: hahahahah
Bum One: hahahaha

116

𝄞𝄞𝄞𝄞𝄞𝄞𝄞𝄞𝄞𝄞𝄞𝄞𝄞𝄞𝄞𝄞
𝄞𝄞𝄞𝄞𝄞𝄞𝄞𝄞𝄞𝄞𝄞𝄞𝄞𝄞𝄞𝄞𝄞
𝄞𝄞𝄞𝄞𝄞𝄞𝄞𝄞𝄞𝄞𝄞𝄞𝄞𝄞𝄞𝄞

Bum Two: hahahahahahahahahaha

Bum Two: hahahahahahahahahaha

Bum Two: hahahahahahahahahaha

Bum Two: hahahahaha**hahahahah**

Bum Two: hahahahaha**h** *oho*

Bum Two: hahahahaha**hahahaha**

Bum Two: hahahahahahahahahahaha

Bum Two: hahahahahahahahahahahaha

Bum Two: hahahahahahahahahahahahahaha

Bum Two: hahahahahahahahahahahahahahaha

Bum Two: hahahahahahahahahahahahahahahaha

Bum Two: hahahahahahahahahahahahahahahahahah

Bum Two: hahahahahahahahahahahaha

Bum Two: hahahahahahaha**hahahahaha**

Bum Two: hahahahahahahah ᵃᵃᵃᵃᵃ

Bum Two: hahahahahahahah ᵃᵃᵃᵃᵃ

Bum Two: hahahahahahaha**hahahahaha**

Bum Two: hahahahahahahahahahahah

Bum Two: hahahahahahahahahahahaha

Bum Two: hahahahahahahahahahahah

Bum Two: hahahaha

Bum Two: hahahaha

Bum Two: hahahaha

Bum Two: hahahaha

Bum Two: hahahaha